Sloane Ryder

The 5 C's Challenge

Copyright © 2016 Sloane Ryder
All rights reserved.
ISBN: 0-9975723-0-2
ISBN-13:   978-0-9975723-0-8

DEDICATION

For my P, whose character has inspired me, whose love has shown me things I have never felt before, and with whom I have had the pleasure to go on this journey.

ACKNOWLEDGMENTS

The day has come where I can publicly acknowledge those who I hold a deep admiration for, for their continued support in my creative process.

Thanks to Trudy, who has depth of insight and interesting knowledge; "Kliney", my friend for life; my family for following me wherever I go; my kids, for making me the mom I am today; and always, my P.

INDEX

"Now what am I to do with my life?" I ask Maria.

It's past five in the evening in Newport, Rhode Island. After a long few days working in the salon together, we are sat in the kitchen enjoying our monthly meal.

"Oh Sammie, surely there must be something you can do with yourself? It's Saturday night and you have no kids."

Maria gestures at my modest but empty home. Her optimism always guides me in the right direction. She is a nurturing soul who took me in as her adopted sister from another mother.

I can be away from her for weeks or even months and when we meet up, we just pick up from where we left off. We've shared many experiences, and created many memories together over the years. We've spent hours in each other's company, laughing at all sorts of silly thoughts and ideas that we've had, such as, what we'd be prepared to do for a million dollars. We would think up all the craziest things we could, to see what our natural instincts or responses would be.

Would you lick vomit for a million dollars? Would you drive a car naked? Would you eat a cupful of flies, worms or beetles? Then of course, we would keep the same things but raise the amounts, seeing if a higher price tag would change our minds.

Another conversation we'd have was coming up with the best, or funniest, porn star names. Some of the classics like Hugh G. Rection or Christi Cream were always favorites. Juvenile banter about Ben Dover, Hugh Jarse or Johnny Depth always made us chuckle. Maria's codename is "Maria Mucho Masturbator" and mine is "Sammie Sucklets." We both have a crude sense of humor, which keeps us amused for hours. We can even finish each other's sentences at the end of the evening, because that's how well we connect with each other, on so many levels.

We would come up with lists of our favorite entertainers, and the people we would love to share a liquid lunch with. My top three would be Justin Timberlake, because he is my mommy crush, and my daughter would tell all her jealous friends at school. Next would be Mick Jagger. Not only because he is one of the most popular and influential front men of rock and roll history, with a charming English accent, but also because of his unique songwriting talent and energetic onstage charisma. My dad is even a fan of this rock legend. Finally, Beyoncé, because of her strong modern-day feminism, and powerful sexy voice. Laughter surrounds our conversations and dreams.

Maria always entertains me with her vibrant personality and spontaneous musings. She has taught me many things about life, but the most important thing is that she will never judge me and will always be accepting of me wherever I may be in life. It's the simple things in life that mean the most, and that's the kind of friendship that I share with her. She's better than a pair of jeans that fits just right. Being with Maria is better than having sex with a lover, because I can trust her totally and never feel threatened. She will never play head games or test our friendship. Never in a million years will she take advantage of our friendship by keeping score of who did what to whom. I can ask a favor and she will do it willingly and never hold it against me. She will never remind me of the things she's done for me, or the number of times she's bailed me out. She's what I call a true friend and I sincerely value our friendship.

I glance around the room at the homemade artwork stuck on the white fridge and scattered pictures of my kids in sports and yearly school photos. Neon plastic tumblers stacked beside the sink. Three lonely cherry wood bar chairs line the kitchen island.

"It feels strange, Maria."

I notice an eerie silence in facing the realization of my new life.

I've been struggling to find my identity since the divorce. The pressure and stress has been getting to me so much that Jason has taken to looking after the kids for an extended period, until I "sort myself out." I didn't expect that my decision to temporarily pass them into his care was going to be so difficult for me. It's one thing to have him out of my life, but quite another not having the kids around.

"Now come on. That isn't the girl that I know. You're always getting into everyone's business and making people smile with your creative talents at the salon," she says. "You transform people. Why don't you transform yourself?"

"Yeah, but look at me now. So much has changed," I mutter.

I catch a glimpse of myself in the reflection of the wall mirror across from me. Damn hair, so limp and lifeless, and needing a retouching at the roots. The grays are starting to show. That cheap everlasting Brightshine family-size shampoo I've been using isn't working. Since my ex has withheld some child support payments, I'm stuck cutting corners and costs, until the next court date. I thought I could get by with the no-frills brands. I guess my hair is the latest sacrifice.

Why can't I have the natural beauty that Christy Brinkley has with her golden highlights kissed by the sun? She's aged well. Why can't I age gracefully with my head held high? I wish I could afford cosmetic surgery to take care of the wrinkles on my forehead. They seem to magically increase with age. Maybe what I should do tonight is take the grays away, and with it, my blues too.

"Sammie, I've got to go. I was supposed to be out the door forty-five minutes ago. Dinner was awesome as usual. But seriously, why don't you redefine yourself and learn what it means to really live your life. That bastard ex-husband is out of your life now. It's time for you to start living again. Be creative and connect with yourself. Do the things that you've always wanted to do, and find the courage to try. It's so tempting to blame yourself. Don't be a victim any longer."

Maria collects her oversized purse and manages to stuff a few more breadsticks into her mouth.

"That's easy for you to say," I reply, as I sit picking at my cuticles.

My hands look like they've aged at least ten years with the umpteen hair washes I've done at the Hair For You salon.

"Are you listening to me? You have to realize what you are in control of," Maria says, as she points to me.

"Yeah, yeah. I know. But I'm not used to this." I glance at the old white plastic wall clock and start to feel guilty.

Maria is always there to pick me up when I need a pep talk. Her words echo in my ears, like a recording of my favorite Rolling Stones song, "Sympathy for the Devil." The repetitious hypnotic sound of the backing vocals on this track makes me question my beliefs and the influence of her angelic charm. Maria sometimes is that angel voice that sits on my shoulder and tells me the right thing to do.

Prolog

You know the kind, the one that influences you and talks common sense. But damn, the second voice, on my other shoulder, is the devil, that sits there and undermines every little positive thought that comes along. Always harboring impure thoughts.

I need a conscience like Maria to keep me balanced. She is my scarecrow and the wisest gal in all of Newport. Dorothy from The Wizard of Oz would listen to the scarecrow, so why shouldn't I? Everybody has to start off from somewhere, even Dorothy.

Now I have the opportunity to restart my life and redefine myself. With a little planning I can get to the place where I want to be. If I stay on a focused course, I will eventually get it right and do the things that I want to do. If I neglect myself in the process and forget to plan, things in life may end up beyond my control. Instead of letting life just happen, I will come up with a plan. A new direction in life, and a new me, is on the menu.

Maria gives me a friendly hug and leaves me to reflect on our latest conversation, her words still ringing in my ears.

She suggested that I be creative and connect. We are from different cultures, and both love food, which is our springboard to living. All good things in life have a cost associated with them.

Hmm… creative, connect, culture, culinary, cost. Maybe I've got something here.

The recipe of The 5 C's Challenge has been born and it's up to me to try to see what I can learn from it!

Let me try these ingredients and see how they can change and improve my life and attitude.

It is Saturday night after all. Surely, I can come up with something!

Recipe for The 5 C's Challenge

Ingredients:

Creativity: I will try things that are new and outside of my comfort zone.

Cost: Everything in life has an associated cost. The price may be emotional, social, physical or economic.

Culinary: My enjoyment of food will be explored in detail. Food can nurture the soul and provide comfort.

Culture: I will experience the world through various social situations to which I am exposed. I will be open to new experiences and try different things.

Connect: I will touch the lives and connect with others in some way, shape or form.

~ Recipe 1 ~
Saturday's Lonely Surprise

Prep time:	One evening
Serves:	One

This recipe will challenge me in five easy steps to tackle the loneliness and boredom I feel now that my world is gone. The ingredients will attempt to address the emptiness of losing two lovely children to a shared custody arrangement with their father. Something new will come if I open the door to opportunity. It is a recipe that will be the beginning to an end of my loneliness.

Creativity:	Write an obituary
Cost:	Couch surf
Culinary:	Eat left over snacks
Culture:	Google a foreign language
Connect:	Call three people

Like the musical group the Smashing Pumpkins song, "The end is the beginning of the end" of my life…

Obituary for Samantha Fleming.
Samantha Angela Fleming, age 47, of Newport, died at 11:45 a.m., November 25, 2015, at the Newport County Courthouse, Rhode Island, when her divorce was finalized. She was born October 11, 1968, in Fort Worth, Texas.

Samantha graduated from Northview High School, before becoming a long time resident of Newport, where she lived since leaving her childhood home of Fort Worth, Texas.

She was a popular hairdresser who loved the clients she met and made beautiful. She enjoyed raising her family, dancing, traveling, playing card games, trying new recipes and visiting garage sales on the weekends.

Surviving her, are her parents, Rose and Francis Martin of Newport; one son, Joshua; one daughter Jessica; one brother, Adam Martin of Seattle; two nephews, Kevin and David Martin, and several cousins.

The visitation is from 9:00 a.m. until 11:00 a.m. on November 28, 2015 at the local funeral home. The funeral service will follow at 11:30 a.m. The burial will be at the Island Cemetery. Memorial contributions may be made to the Make a Wish Foundation and The American Heart Association.

Samantha's dreams were deferred and are now officially dead. Like the great Lorraine Hansberry wrote, inspired by the words of Langston Hughes poem "A Dream Deferred," Samantha died a sad and awful death of an ignored dream. Her condition never seemed to be improved. Samantha was a woman who was not willing to be herself and pursue her own potential dream, and was left lonely. She rarely strayed from the safe path along her journey. She neglected her own needs, always putting others first. Samantha was a great mother who abandoned herself, losing her soul and her identity. She tried to discover herself, however in her attempts, she forgot about her morals and values. In the end, Samantha gave up on life and living.

OK, so now Samantha Fleming is officially "creatively" dead, that ingredient is done and checked off. Let's put her in a casket for the evening and do some much needed couch surfing.

Oh, fuck it! What's on the damn tube tonight? It's been ages since I last watched uninterrupted TV without hearing SportsCenter or Austin and Ally. Time to get comfy on the cream and blue floral sectional couch and onto the next ingredient. My recipe won't be hard to complete by the end of the evening and I can feel… Damn! I don't know what to feel anymore.

The next ingredient, "Culinary." Time to reduce, reuse and make space. I will make a grand effort at eating all bags of leftover snacks that are already opened. Let's see what I have lying on the counter. Benn's potato chips. They are very tasty, and once you start munching them, it's hard to stop. I pick up and try to eat a stale chip that has been there forever. OK, so that won't work. Let me try tortilla chips as they are bound to be a hit. But it isn't Cinco de Mayo and I don't have any tequila shots or margaritas with salt to chase it with, and the salsa in the fridge looks like a science project with mold growing over it, that no one has touched for weeks. Why don't I just throw this stuff away? I obviously can't keep up with the stuff on the counter, which keeps piling up. Well, I guess I can skip this recipe ingredient and move on to the next one. Some things in life you have to adapt and sometimes you can't control what elements already exist.

Since there is nothing on TV and the snacks aren't making the list, I'll move on to the next ingredient. Time to boot up my laptop, with the letter M key that still sticks after something was dropped onto the keyboard, and Google German phrases and practice saying them. I took two years of German in high school, mainly so I could sit next to Derek Phillips. He was born to be a leader and a great skier. I remember him to this day with his dark wavy hair and bright blue eyes. He looked like he could just float down the Swiss Alps. He was one of the tallest boys in the class and was good at everything he touched. He had muscles that could compete with a professional bodybuilder, and I always thought he would make great babies with his genetics and perfect bright white teethy smile.

What to type in? Let's start with, I'm alone on a Saturday night. Ich bin allein an einem Samstag abend. OK, let me try speaking it.

"Ich bin a lime an enem sam stag a bend." No, that doesn't sound quite right. Next one. Do you have a fast red BMW that I can drive on the autobahn? Haben sie einen schnellen red BMW, dass ich auf der autobahn fahren? I'm lost and I can't find it. Ich bin verloren und ich kann es nicht finden. Let's see if I can look at myself in the mirror and repeat these phrases. Oh dear, this is harder than I thought.

Eek, look at those wrinkles on my forehead. When did I get those? It must've been last week when I was at the grocery store, picking up those half price dented cans of vegetables off the clearance shelf. Look at those laugh lines along my cheeks. It's worse than the Joker from Batman. But I don't think I'm laughing now. That stark white face and ghoulish smile has almost become my face. But my ax to grind isn't with Batman or the way that I look. It's with my lost identity. My own life has become my archenemy. Where is the hero that rises above all this? Maybe if I had a permanent grin I could face life that way. Even in the movies the Joker has had many faces, from Jack Nicholson, my personal favorite, to Heath Ledger, who's untimely death cast a shadow on all that followed.

Before I call it an evening, I've one last ingredient to complete for my Saturday's Lonely Surprise, and that is to "Connect." Call three people on the spur of the moment to get together for a drink. This should be interesting! Who do I have on my mobile phone call list?

The first person that I can think of is my dad. My father, Francis. Like the ex-coach of the Indianapolis Colts, a respected, classy and hardworking gentleman, who taught his team so many life lessons on the field and off. He showed his team that you can win in all kinds of ways. He believed the team should have a thought process, a philosophy and the conviction to stick with it. My dad has served to do the same, but with a cigar in his hands at all times. What five words would I use to describe him? Hardworking, distant, strong, stoic and stubborn. Well, maybe the last one is more genetic than I thought. I think stubbornness runs in the family. I will dial him up anyway. I'm not sure I can just call him without a reason. He will think something is wrong or that I need something. He might even be asleep at this time. Usually after watching the ten o'clock weather report he goes to bed.

"Hello?" he answers in his familiar tone.

"Hi Dad," I say, waiting for his response.

"Hi Sammie. What do you need?" he asks.

"I don't need anything right now," I reply defensively.

"What do you mean you don't need anything? Are you OK?"

"Yes Dad, I'm fine."

I start to feel like I'm being overly sensitive, when I really just need his support. That child-like feeling of standing in front of Dad, asking for his permission to go to a friend's sleepover, runs over me. Then Dad accuses me of wearing too much make-up or that my black skirt is too short and tight, but I am determined to wear it anyway, and sneak out of the house thinking he will never catch me. Those memories and feelings come over me like a fast approaching wave at the Narragansett Town Beach.

"Alright, so why are you calling?"

"I just wanted to talk to you," I say in a crisis of conviction.

"What about? Are the kids alright? Did your car break down again?"

"No Dad. I was just wondering if you wanted to stop by for some coffee or something?"

"Do you know what time it is?"

"Uh?"

"It's after ten. You sound strange. You weren't at that neighbor's house were you?"

"No Dad. It doesn't matter, just forget it. I gotta go. Sorry to have bothered ya! Goodnight Dad."

I don't believe it! The chorus from Coldplay's "The Scientist" echoes in my mind as I hang up the phone. All I wanted from him was for once in his life to tell me he loved me and had time for just me. Not me and the kids, or me and the family, just little sad 'ol me. I would be Daddy's girl all over again with a big goofy smile on my face, and my heart would beat once again.

Let me try the next person on my list. My friend and work colleague, Guy Rinker. We met at hairdressing school and have ended up working at the same salon together. He leads an interesting life to say the least. He's the stereotypical tall, thin, well-dressed gay guy that's every females' friend. He has blonde highlights and is up on all the latest fashion trends. He has a creative side and artistic flare that nurtures any woman's self-image with the stroke of a brush. He has the heart of an angel and the hands of a true blooded passionate artist. He will sacrifice time away from his lover so that he can finish making his magic. He can look at a woman from a dual perspective and know exactly what her man wants her to look like inside his sexy bedroom. What talent that is! Since he has no ulterior motive to bang her and have her suck his cock, he satisfies his clients with artistic genius while earning some greenbacks. He can always give an honest assessment of a woman's looks by saying, "Darling, you look absolutely fabulous," and really mean it. I dial the phone. It rings three times. Not a good sign. I think to myself, it's Saturday night and only losers with no social life are standing by their phone waiting for a call from Samantha. I don't leave a message for fear of sounding desperate. If he does have caller id, I'll just say that it was a mistakenly harmless butt dial, as I was having so much fun on my couch. Two strikes so far.

Next friend to ask for coffee on the spur of the moment is Rosie, my old roommate from when I was a waitress at the local restaurant. I've not seen her in a while, and it would be nice to catch up.

Rosie is always good for a great tongue wagging. She knows pop culture like the back of her hand and can talk about any subject. I would nominate her to be on any quiz show. I dial the phone and it immediately goes to the answering machine. This time I leave a message.

"Hey Rosie, what's up? Samantha here. I know you're probably off rocking with some dude, but give me a jingle some time. I would love to catch ya! Later."

Well, not a 100% successful attempt at reaching the best combination of the 5 C's Challenge, but at least I've started, and given it a go. Tomorrow is another day, with new challenges to set myself. I yawn, and fall asleep on the lonely couch.

~ Recipe 2 ~
Sunday's Boredom Breakthrough

Prep time:	One day
Serves:	One

This recipe will allow a connection with others in five easy steps. It brings broader horizons with a hint of diversity. It will take a bite out of dealing with the guilt and self-doubt that has been encountered in connecting with others. I will explore new interests while adding depth to the old ones. This will surely add spice to my life and break my normal routine. Throw out some inhibitions and add extra people to make the moment last longer with a bold new flavor. This will also allow all my feelings of loneliness to cool down, and heat things up in my life.

Creativity:	Draw a picture
Cost:	Smoke a cigar
Culinary:	Eat one type of food
Culture:	Kiss a stranger
Connect:	Facebook

I want to do things on my own, discover the world around me, and not be afraid. I've heard of Erickson's psychosocial development taking into perspective feelings of autonomy versus shame and doubt. Do I have the ability to realize self-control? Remember that self-doubt is sometimes a defense mechanism the brain uses when it feels vulnerable. Have I done the right things in my life?

Boom! It hits me that I'm no longer Mrs. anything anymore. For the rest of my entire life I'll now be a Ms. and what does that stand for? My daughter's friends will now all address me as Ms. Will I have to make new friends? Should I still associate with the friends of my ex and his family? Will they disown me now, because we are no longer married? Am I now officially off the list of the couple's gatherings, now that I'm a lonely single middle-aged woman? What has happened to me? The girl that I once knew, who was filled with adventure and curiosity, has left. My church envelopes and bank statements will all be changed to Ms. from now. Oh God, what have I done? Where is my identity?

My son has Facebook and all this technology thing under his belt and mastered, but I can't seem to figure it out. It took me forever to figure out how to work my settings and set up a profile. Even coming out of the starting gate I'm already 217 friends behind my son. My own friend-list is few and sparse at best with a mere fifteen people and most of them happen to be blood relatives.

Today's recipe of The 5 C's Challenge for "Connect" is to add ten new friends to my Facebook. It can't be that hard even if I have been out of the loop. I'm no doubt ready to type as I sit in front of my laptop.

OK, so let's find some new friends. Well since I didn't get Rosie by phone, let me try to surprise her by Facebooking her. I will try Guy Rinker too while I'm at it.

Well, I already feel desperate. Let me expand my list a bit more. My neighbor, I haven't tried him yet, William Mathews. He's like my second dad. I know his family like my own. He's always outside when I have to shovel the snow from the driveway or rake the leaves in the Fall. He will help me check the oil in my car or fill my tires with air. Jokingly, I could list all his handy instructions on my resume of life. He has taught me many valuable life lessons, like how to patch a wall with plaster or check my gutters for leaves. I can always count on him to give me a hand. He is sincere and honest, and shares stories about his kid's getting high powered jobs even without a college degree, or his grandkids. He gives me advice even better than Dad. He says that men aren't complicated creatures. They only care about three things: food, television and sex. I know that I didn't get it right with my ex-husband. I'm glad that I have my neighbor around when things don't work out in my own life.

I'm sure William would love to have me as a Facebook friend. Holy Shit! He has 335 friends listed on his Facebook page. I didn't know he had such an active social life. I do feel like a loser now! Even my neighbor has more of a life than I do!

I type in some more. Let me think of some reliable and trustworthy people who I know won't say no. Mary Whitaker comes to mind. She is a great cook, always organizing church dinners and Bible discussions. She goes to my local church, although I know I haven't been to it in ages, since the kids had confirmation. Her style is always classic and her hairstyle never changes with her tight, pulled back auburn hair. I don't think she would even turn on the organist with that look. Let me have a drink to that one. I pour myself a nice glass of chianti, even if it is only noon. Wait a minute! I haven't had a spot of communion wine in ages. I chuckle to myself.

I know! I haven't typed my own brother's name. I hesitate at the thought of reaching out to Adam. I've so many walls to consider. We sort of lost touch for a while and never really connected after I started having kids. Since he moved to Seattle, he is even more distant. He never seems interested in what I'm doing and he seems too busy with driving his white Escalade around town. The only time he will call me is when he's waiting to pick up his kids from school or on his way to an important meeting. He never stops and calls me as a priority. He always criticizes how I raise the kids and makes comments about my colorful friends. Sometimes it seems like we are always in competition with each other, rather than admiring each other's talents. I wouldn't outwardly admit that I'm jealous of him, but I know that I am. Sometimes, I feel that Dad approves of him more than me. He seems to praise him more for his achievements. Adam is more successful in life than I will ever be. He has a college degree and a high-powered job in an office. No matter how hard I try, I can never measure up to my Dad's expectations or Adam's accomplishments. But what the heck. Cheers to him! Let me have a drink to that decision. Typing "Adam Martin." There are at least a dozen that come up. Let's see if I can narrow it down to him! It's quite difficult to do when people don't post their face as a profile picture.

Searching through my head, why don't I just randomly think of people? How about my regular customer who comes in every two weeks on a Thursday for a haircut? Paul Walsh, he's never at a loss of words. I add him to my list.

Let me think. I can't get Derek Phillips out of my head, so why don't I try him. I can't get the thought of those deep blue eyes which melted me when he stared straight at me and smiled, with that fake tan and weather forecaster smile. I wish I could have known more than his smile because as I sit here desperate, I wonder what he would look like in the flesh. The thought of him without a shirt and seeing his tan broad shoulders is sending me chills. I feel like a schoolgirl all over again and get giddy with excitement. I'm pathetic!

This is proving harder than I thought, especially when this wine is going down like grape juice on a hot day. I pour myself another glass of red, and sit sipping it until I can think of a few more names. Maybe when it comes down to it, I've been too busy with my kid's lives to think about my own. Let me dig deep for the final three.

Pete Valaquez, was someone I knew from the high school production of "Anything Goes," who now lives in New Orleans, so I'm told. But what if he finds me boring and decides not to "friend" me? How will I deal with the rejection? His gorgeous green eyes are something I'll never forget. I was more than desperate for him in high school. It was more than just a crush. I had several sexual fantasies about him. My ultimate fantasy would be him dominating me in numerous hot and sexy positions. The Kama Sutra would take over and we would try every extraordinary position. He would drive me insane with a series of hot pleasures. From the fantastic "Rocking Horse" to the classic "Nirvana," we would try all those erotic positions. Pete would meet all my needs and fetishes. I would savor every moment, being clenched around him and feeling him deep inside me and filling me up with his hot cum. He would fuck me over and over again, his hips grinding and thrusting against me, while his rigid tight abs would be pressed against my erect breasts. His entire body would be insanely hard and we would make primitive love-making noises. Plunging hard and fast, our hot sex would break us out into a divine sweat of animal magnitude. Orgasms would flow as he reached the spots that ache for his manhood. Images of his sexy body and my unfulfilled fantasies left me feeling breathless, and allowed me to believe that someday I would be wanted.

Another name? Jennifer Brand, the mother of my daughter's friend who always has a perfect manicure of false nails. She smokes like a chimney and is a size four but eats Peeps as a meal.

For now, the final name to Facebook is Dawn Fry, my boss at work. She has a passive-aggressive manner, so in many ways our relationship can be a battleground of sorts. Sometimes I have to bite my tongue while dealing with her sarcastic comments. She thinks that she can make me stop whatever I'm doing to sort out her problems and whims. I really wish I had the nerve to tell her to get stuffed and tell her what she can do with all her power. But why not? I can play her game and pretend to be her friend too. Isn't that what it is about pretending, and creating false relationships, to get where you want in life? The problem is, how can you tell where you stand with all the blurred lines that are everywhere in the work place? The empty bottle of red wine says, "What the hell!" That challenge was a little harder than I thought but I managed to get it done.

The phone rings.

Damn the room is spinning. I'm in a physically and emotionally disastrous state of intoxication. What if it's someone important on the phone? They will know something is up if I don't answer, and probably will as soon as I do.

"Hiya! Ooh, what can I do for ya?" I ask in the best calm voice I can muster, as I pick up the phone.

"Honey, is that you?" Dad asks.

"Oh Daddy, oh, I umm, ah, ah, yeah it's terrible, just terrible! I have this list, right? And I just can't get the list right! You know that list that I made? And no, I think that no one will love me, and I won't have any friends at all." I respond, not making a damn bit of sense under the influence of alcohol.

"Honey, Have you been drinking? You don't sound so hot."

"What d'ya mean hot? I'm not hot at all. I don't even have the heat on in this place, but where did I put my…?" I mutter.

"Honey, are the kids with you?"

"What? Oh yeah, no. I don't know, wait, they are with um…" I reply.

"As long as they are OK. You know you really shouldn't drink like this! I don't know what has gotten into you. Call me tomorrow. Your mother worries about you."

Click. The phone call ends. Even though the room is spinning, I know he won't be pleased. He can never deal with confrontation. Maybe that's where I learned it from.

Anyway, I'm hungry! I've a case of the munchies, so I'm going to do something about my uneasiness and annoyance. What better way to deal with my problems than to move to my next challenge, which is to eat lots of one food. I find comfort in food and turn to it when things are rough. Knowing that I'll never be a size four, I keep up the carbs. So for the next twenty-four hours, I decide that I'm just going to eat potatoes. Fried, mashed, baked, boiled. First, I will have them as hot, greasy and slightly crisp french fries, my favorite! Tomorrow for breakfast I will make hash browns with lots of ketchup. I will maybe have potato salad for lunch with lots of mayo, celery and hard-boiled eggs. I just love potatoes! It's amazing how many different varieties of food one little potato can make. How versatile they are! I could write a whole cookbook with potato recipes if I was really adventurous! I feel like I could do anything, in the kitchen, at least. Maybe the Chianti has really gotten to my brain. I've a list of things I feel I can accomplish. These wine goggles are really powerful.

I do hate feeling that I let Dad down. I should make it up to him by drawing a picture for him, just like I used to do each year. I always loved making him homemade Father's Day cards. What age did that end? I can't remember when the last one was. I wonder if he's kept any of my cards. When was I more interested in boys than giving hugs to my dad? It makes me feel sad thinking that those days are now gone.

I know, I will draw him a charcoal picture image, then he will forgive me. So, I reach for the drawer to get blank paper and pencils, and with black charcoal in hand, I show my creative side. I once made a beach scene of Newport as my first real drawing for him. Dad always boasted about how much he loved the resort town as it had something for everyone. The historic architecture, unique boutiques which my mom loved, and a place to relax near the water is what ignited his spirit. Life seemed much more simple back then.

Quickly, I make a variety of different lines in a silhouette. It is a familiar image, but one that constantly changes before my eyes. Smudging the vine charcoal with my fingertips, I am eager to get my desired effect. Using a variety of techniques, I press hard and soft to make the image to my liking. Holding the stick in my hand, I use my thumb and forefinger with my palm facing the surface of the paper to get the proper grip. I manipulate the kneaded eraser like clay to create highlights and blend the lines. Applying less pressure and going out of the lighted areas, the picture takes form, becoming more realistic and visible. Perhaps not a big life changing revelation, but a simple act of love. A face-splitting and genuine smile comes over my face.

Our family was never rich enough for a yacht, but baby, we could secretly dream together! The panoramic coastal views along scenic Ocean Drive are breathtaking. I remember having a picnic with the family at Brenton Point State Park. I never laughed so hard, as the birds were circling around trying to eat our bologna sandwiches. The majestic vistas of the Atlantic Ocean as it meets Narragansett Bay were always a calming force for me. Unfortunately, my attempts at kite flying weren't always successful, as my princess kite would never stay up long enough in the air to catch the high ocean winds.

During my childhood, Dad always made me secretly proud when he would hang up my artwork in the kitchen. Now that I'm older, I wonder if he will do the same with my new drawing for him, a silhouette of me, plain 'ol Sammie.

I decide that my next challenge will be to smoke a cigar. It won't cause lung cancer if I have just one, right? The sound of practicing on sucking long and hard on a dark thing filled with white stuff, makes me feel very naughty. I know Dad wouldn't approve. I haven't done that sort of thing before. I happen to know that there is one left over from when my ex used to play Texas Holdem with his friends in the basement. Since I have the impulse, I search for it. I remember that he kept them in the desk drawer where he used to pay bills.

The anticipation of feeling a long, thin cigar between my fragile fingers gets my panties wet. I imagine what it would be like to try different varieties, like a smaller stubbly one. Who knew that there were so many shapes with so many names? Pyramid, Robusto, Torpedo and Perfecto. Maybe I should rush out and buy a Hemingway cigar. The tastes are varied with spicy, sweet, burnt, cocoa, roasted, aged, nutty, creamy, chewy, fruity, and leathery flavors. I think I've stumbled upon a new adventure and all of a sudden I want them all. The only reason I know this is because my ex falsely tried to impress others with his cigar aficionado talk. I could try a Cohiba cigar that was originally made for Fidel Castro. It sounds very tempting and crossing the line. All my past must have rubbed off of my memory. I imagine different heads and different pleasures that I would enjoy, each one giving a different sensation.

After finding what I was looking for, I stare at it, and then hold it like a cock that I haven't experienced in a while. I've a smoldering desire to put it in my mouth. I touch the length and gaze at it.

I enjoy looking at the Corona and open foot, which I can't wait to light with my flame. I'm eager with anticipation, rolling it between my fingers, enjoying its length and diameter. I run my nose along its edge, smelling the sweet tobacco aroma. This is something I've never done before and I feel a little nervous. The ritual of handling a cigar is a strange experience to the uninitiated. Holding it between my middle finger and forefinger, I put my pink lips together engulfing the tip. I gently squeeze it to make sure it isn't too firm or soft. I like that the feeling is just the right texture. I close my eyes and know that this is the one. I'm a virgin cigar smoker. Using a long wooden flame, I light the open foot and purse my lips on the closed head. I engage in a little foreplay with my cigar. I warm the tobacco in the foot of the cigar savoring the moment.

I'm careful to hold the flame below the foot without touching it, gradually rotating the cigar a few times until the foot is evenly warmed. I've set it up for the perfect experience. The long shaft is warmed up and easier to light. My lips feel soft and wrap around it. I inhale slowly and suck so deep like it is my first time giving a blowjob. My lips quiver in eager anticipation. I slow up a little bit to make sure it's lit. My heart beats a little faster. Cough, cough. Eww, I wasn't ready for the rush that goes to my head. The thick heavy smoke surprises me.

I draw on the cigar again, holding the smoke in my mouth for a few seconds, trying to savor the taste. Let me try sucking again, because I want to master this. I realize it's an odd occurrence for a woman to smoke a cigar. But why? Sharon Stone, Whoopi Goldberg, Demi Moore and Madonna have all smoked in public, and I'm not even half as sexy as them. I suck again, while wondering whether smoking really will make me feel more sexy. This time I exhale deeply, puckering my lips in a circle and blow the smoke out. I close my eyes to feel the sensations that are rushing to my head. The flavor is intense and mind-blowing. I smile in excitement that I'm able to smoke it now without choking or coughing. I'm a fast learner. I try again and reposition my fingers, getting a better grip. I feel like I'm manipulating the cigar into a better position. I inhale and exhale with a rhythm and flow. My lips form a circular shape as I blow gently but firmly. I'm getting the long drag and slow flow action. The quick burn signals that I must cherish our time together. I'm now feeling more at ease and less tense. I don't know if it's a trendy thing, but a mother of two in her forties would never be caught doing this in my town. It seems rather taboo in nature. I love the idea that anyone can do it and that thrills me. Why can't I put my mouth around a good Cuban? It is rather unexpected, but right now I really don't give a damn and I will do what I want, when I want. I'm ready to experience the ultimate climax.

My blue eyes follow the length of the cigar. As I exhale I move the long firm cigar away from my mouth, and turn to look at the ash that I've created on the tip. A devilish grin fills my face. Why should men have all the fun? I practice different positions with my mouth and lightly hold the end with my teeth. The oral stimulation means I don't have to bond with it, just put it aside when I'm done. I'm in control and feel selfishly guilty. The oral sensation is such a tease to my senses. I want to feel a pleasurable spot. Maybe I'm a born natural and I never knew it was in me. That gets me excited and I feel a tingly proud sensation for feeling so bad. The feelings are intense and pleasurable. I try to not let my tongue get in the way of the movement of my lips. I slowly suck in and blow out. I tilt my head and even try to make a smoke ring. Hmm, I'm getting too confident and ahead of myself. I amaze myself that I can add spice to my life, and have been able to breakaway from my normal routine with this challenge.

I haven't been out in a long time and I'm going stir crazy in this box of a home. While I'm up for adventure, it's about time for me to get out and explore the nightlife.

Rosie always goes on about the nightlife in Newport. She told me of the times when she would stay out until the early hours of the morning on Thames Street, hanging around the bars. She would go out after working her shift during the week and enjoy watching Johnny Jacobs perform his light-hearted style of musical entertainment. She would be a regular fixture, like a groupie on a Tuesday night, ordering her favorite drink, "Sex on the Beach", or she would see how many drinks she could have bought for her during the course of the evening.

Suddenly, like a lost person going to college for the first time and meeting my new dorm roommate, I find myself arriving at a crowded club. A band are setting up and the room is noisy. This makes the idea of a newbie like me easy to blend in without too much awkwardness. I head for the bar and order a Corona with lime. I look down at my frumpy clothing and notice my floral print top with white buttons and baggy jeans that I bought in the '80s and never replaced. This outfit looks like it could have matched my grandma's curtains. It may not have been the best selection for capturing the eyes of stranger.

I take a long drink and get set to meet my match for the evening, noticing a man in the corner with a six foot muscular build and glistening ivory teeth on a black background. The shiny gold cross around his neck makes me think that he isn't a serial killer. His thick eyebrows remind me of an image of Shemar Moore from the "Young and the Restless". I can see the contours of his muscles against the tight white cotton t-shirt that he's wearing with his dark blue denim jeans. He notices that I'm staring at him like a schoolgirl being asked a history question in first period, and raises a smile. I don't let my lack of confidence and inexperience get in the way of my latest challenge.

I take the plunge even deeper and smile back, moving into his territory. The band begins to play, and the sound of their music encourages me to dance his dance. It fills my senses with a carefreeness and anything is OK in this moment. I take a deep breath and move towards a free seat next to him.

He looks directly at me with hazel eyes that read my thoughts.

"You new in this town? I haven't seen you here before?"

"What gave it away?"

A slow awkward nervous smile encompasses me.

He nods at me and moves closer than the acceptable limits of personal space that I'm normally used to.

"So how does this normally go?" I boldly ask, knowing that I'm clearly out of my territory and need a map to navigate my next move.

There isn't a GPS that can guide me through the next phase. Life would be so much easier if there was, as I wouldn't make too many wrong turns or decisions, and if I did, it would just recalculate and tell me the right direction to go. I would even take an old fashioned map at this point, or better still a treasure map.

I could follow the dotted lines until I got to my personal treasure. I would love to see what's inside his big treasure box. I'm sure he has treasure fit for a queen.

I don't know my limits. It isn't like we've just met at a wedding and I can get away with just becoming intimate with a stranger while having lots of drinks running from the champagne fountain. His attraction and unexpected diversity makes me feel like a horny schoolgirl. I'm vulnerable and weak in his presence. It's something new and exhilarating, which gives me a thrill. The unknown is an untapped resource that I haven't fed into previously.

"How do you want it to go?"

He taps his long fingers in rhythm to the music, and then reaches towards me and touches the right side of my cheek. I'm in disbelief that he even gave me a hint of a look.

I take another swig of my drink and looking directly at him say, "My daddy would never believe that I'm talking to a man like you."

"Well, maybe we should do more than just talk," he suggests.

My heart beats strongly in anticipation as he moves closer to me, and I can feel the heat of his breath kissing my face in this smoky room. His nose slides against mine and his face moves across my eyeline. I realize he's within a lip distance of my rose red lips. I lean towards him in anticipation, like a movie scene running through my head of "Pretty Woman." I'm Julia Roberts standing on a fire escape leaning in to my stranger prince who is here to rescue me from my life. The music plays in the background. The lights shine on me, and I'm the star of the movie capturing the man who is going to save me from my reality.

A fiery heat rushes through me and I can feel my breasts automatically pushing out to him to get his attention and approval. A surge of excitement rushes to my white panties as I close my eyes. The smell of rum and coke chased down by the classic scent of his fragrant cologne kisses my nose. His sweet hard lips push toward the welcome arrival of my quivering giddy mouth. His lips touch mine and we share a firm, long passionate kiss. The kiss ignites all of my inner cravings. He is perfect in presentation and style. All I can think about is accommodating my needs and desires.

His firm hand touches my left ear and glides along my curly hairline. His fingertips press along my neck and run down to my shoulders. I move closer to him signaling my highest approval. My eyes meet his and I'm under his spell. Then, in a brief moment of lucidity, I realize that I've just joined the ranks of all the other women who have fallen to the player's routine. But this time, he's been awarded a frumpy soccer mom housewife who is out of her league.

A moment of great doubt enters my mind. In panic and desperation, I quickly turn to find an escape. The nearest exit is in the corner of the room. The band are playing a loud guitar solo, patrons clapping their hands in the air. I turn my head and stumble past empty cups and dancing couples. This isn't right. I'm not ready. Before I can win another stare and be melted by his delicious smile, I run for the door to grab the pure air that wasn't filling my lungs before. My inhibitions have been conquered and the challenge of kissing a stranger has been completed.

~ Recipe 3 ~
Learning To Say Goodbye To Me

Prep time:	Two days
Serves:	One or more

This recipe brings a willingness to try new experiences and adventures. Learning to make space for the feelings that will lead to a new lifestyle of change. No faith or tears are needed to say goodbye to the old me.

Creativity:	Design clothing
Cost:	Drastic haircut
Culinary:	Kill an animal
Culture:	Dance
Connect:	Take a course

Oh God, I need to do something positive with my life after a crazy Sunday night. Reading articles in the Newport Daily News, I see that the American Red Cross is running free CPR classes this afternoon at the local library on Spring Street. Maybe a mission of saving others will give my life purpose and meaning. Life-saving techniques can be of admirable use to anyone caught in a life-threatening situation. I phone and check that I can just turn up and participate. I'm told that I'm more than welcome to turn up, anytime from 12:30 p.m. onward.

I arrive shortly after 12:45 p.m. and am directed to the Lower Level Program Room, a largish room, with a raised stage over which an American Red Cross flag is hanging. I'm warmly greeted by one of the volunteers, identified by their red jackets with emblems and identity cards attached, who leads me to Annie, and explains and demonstrates when and how to perform CPR. I'm advised that the first thing I should do is phone 911, and then that I should do hands-only CPR until the ambulance arrives. I'm shown the technique of how to hold my hands, where to place them, and how firmly and often I need to compress the chest. The rapid pace of giving chest compressions seems second nature but the thought of having to do this to a stranger in a real life situation seems quite daunting. It's a good thing my manikin Annie is not really living and breathing. Through practice and repetition, I feel that I've mastered it and feel comfortable with my newly acquired skills. Let's hope I never have to use them!

After learning and practicing my new skills I want to get some fresh air, and move onto my next challenge. Maybe a drive north via Portsmouth, and across the river will do me some good. I check that I have relevant proofs of I.D. with me, do a quick search and route selection on my GPS, and set off. Feelings of nervous excitement flood my mind as I consider my current intentions.

As I travel towards my destination, I spot the beautiful rich vibrant colors of the stained glass windows and large cross at Saint Hubert's Roman Catholic Church. I can't remember the last time I prayed. Maybe praying on the run is what I'm left to do these days, if at all. I know my mind is engaged, but I'll make note to include my heart. I know I'm not with the Lord as he intends me to be. My attention isn't always with Him. Looking at the cross, I know He follows me. He still loves me no matter what. Perhaps, this is what unconditional love is all about. I could fuck up royally and I would still be loved by Him. I don't know why I do what I do. I'm on auto-pilot, just wanting to get there, somewhere. What is my destination and where am I heading? God has given me the gift of life, but I'm not sure I'm worthy of the gift of faith anymore. I feel that I've lost myself and my identity through the divorce process. A middle-aged woman lost without direction. Where is the good in myself these days? I ask the Lord for forgiveness, and continue my journey north, over the Sakonnet River Bridge, and then change direction, heading south, down Route 77 until I reach Lakeside Farm.

I arrive at my destination, and stepping out of the car I begin getting butterflies in my stomach, as I walk around the perimeter of the building looking for the entrance. Entering the store, I gaze in curiosity and fascination at the range of guns on display. I've always wanted to hold one in my hands. The long barrel and shaft are powerful yet sexy. The idea of feeling the barrel and loading it with actual real bullets, fills me with a sense of empowerment. Like a pole dancer trying to sell Girl Scout cookies door to door, I know I don't belong. Feeling like a fish out of water is an understatement, but I'm here now, and I'm not about to turn back. Being a thrifty customer, I want one that's versatile and can get the job done, at a price within my budget. It has to be comfortable to hold, like the feeling of holding a hard cock in the dark. When you hold it right, it feels good in your hands. I find one that's relatively short, wide cartridge, with straight walls, and operates at a low pressure. I feel a wet sensation in my pussy as I think of the enormous stopping power at short range. Although it might have limited range and limited penetration of the shot, it has high stopping power, even if someone like me doesn't know my own limits. I'm told that when the safety is showing red it's ready to fire. I can feel the butt stock leaning on me and it feels so damn good. It's ready to blow. I love the slide release. The feeling is something I could do over and over. I love the feeling of deep penetration as it gives me a thrill. After discussing my requirements with the proprietor, I choose to hire a basic shotgun, over a Muzzleloader. Not like the one Elmer Fudd used on Bugs Bunny. I also hire a shotgun case, limiter plug, eye and ear protection, fluorescent orange safety clothing, and ammunition.

January is mid-way through the hunting season in Rhode Island. I'm told that the wildlife management area has an abundance of game, which should make for a clear and easy target. My mind flashes to the point of what I'm heavily contemplating. The consequences of shooting a defenseless whitetail deer, identifiable by their small ears, white-tipped tail and seasonal gray coat gives me the Catholic guilt that I've become accustomed to whenever I think of doing something wrong. Is this something that I should really be considering? Doubt is something that never stops. I thought this challenge would be something easy.

It shouldn't be too difficult for someone whose only offense was speeding on my way home from the beach three summers ago. The cost of a successful kill would be easy on my wallet, but is that really the price of what a dead deer is worth? I try to console and convince myself that the deer are plentiful in number, and that they need culling in order to prevent over-population.

This shotgun is the most powerful weapon that I've ever held. My hands hold the key to an animal's life or death. If I was Angelina Jolie as Lara Croft trying on guns for size, would I be sexier? Would it gain the approval of others? The reality is that I choose to live off the meat that will nourish me and fill my empty stomach. I don't have a problem purchasing it ready prepared from a store shelf. Selecting my own fresh meat this way, just seems like a step up the food supply chain, cutting out the middle-man.

Gazing at the youth model shotgun, it fits my smaller frame. A twelve gauge is the perfect match for deer hunting. The shotgun is like anything "an inch shorter makes a lot of difference." Although in the bedroom, I'm not sure that motto applies. Many people brag that size matters. The power to drive it home and follow through is what also matters. There a number of deer and wild birds roaming the field. Dressed in fluorescent, I find a vantage point from which to view my prey. I see some small pheasants scamper in the background, although I think that hitting a small moving target would be a lot more difficult than I imagine. In the distance behind the barren trees, I spot a young deer eating. May the good Lord willing and the creeks don't rise, I want to get this right. OK, let me get my mind into this. Slowly and graceful, I take my stance ready to shoot my target. I cannot think of Bambi at times like this, so I think of Jason, my ex. Every time I think of that fucker it makes my blood boil. Prior to the commencement of our acrimonious divorce proceedings, we had taken the hunter safety and education training courses, in order to obtain the necessary hunting permits. Needless to say, the divorce put any hunting on the back-burner.

Taking aim with my gun, feeling the increasing pace and pressure of my heartbeat, I firmly squeeze the trigger and feel it explode. I see the confused innocent eyes of the doe staring back at me after missing my target, before it swiftly flees into the foliage. Further attempts during the course of the day yield no success. It's not the aphrodisiac I thought it would be. I'm not cut out for this. I'm too much of a wimp and have no accuracy. There's no beginners luck in this case. I decide that I can't do this and I will return home hungry and defeated. I accept that I have my limits. Thank God for burger joints!

I return my hired products to the store, and leave empty-handed.

On my return journey I once again pass Saint Hubert's Church, its colorful stained glass windows now illuminated by the buildings internal lighting, contrasting the darkened skies surrounding it. Penance isn't a bad idea after all. But I don't know if all my sins can be forgiven, even by my God. After the emotionally battering experience of failing that challenge, I decide to unwind and regroup. My conscience can be my own worst enemy. Sometimes through disappointment, failure and rejection, I learn the lessons of life and how to handle adversity. True character is determined in those moments, in how I handle these intense situations. There isn't always a play, book or advice column for getting it right. Sure, experience and guidance from a coach would help. But who is the coach and master of my life? Will I learn lessons better through multiple disappointments and failure? A person's choices and decisions impact their future. Winning and conquering at any cost isn't what life is about. It's how you treat others in the process, or by learning to lose gracefully. The superficial gratification of winning is not lost on my kids who understand what teamwork, hard work and dedication truly mean. I think hard about my kids and how I raise them. Reflecting on Jess' and Josh's soccer games that they've played and the bitter disappointments they've faced, I can feel proud how they have handled losing and adversity. Sport allows growth, challenge and development. My kids are learning how to handle life situations through sport. When the other team show up with personalized names on their matching soccer gear and beat their opposition ten to one, my kids still play their little hearts out to the bitter end. They never give up. My kids manage to keep their heads held high. They enjoy the true meaning of the game, which is not purely measured in terms of medals and championships. My kids have taught me how to live my own life. Why don't I feel like holding my head up high now? I should rejoice that I didn't end up killing an animal or hurting the environment for my own selfish pleasure.

I need to clear my mind after my intense struggle in the wild, with a nice relaxing bath and to focus on me. I need to calm down and regroup. I soak, unwind, and try to think of new ways that I can improve myself. I consider a lifestyle change and wonder how I'll feel saying goodbye to the old me. I want to be a butterfly and be able to fly, but right now I feel like I'm a crawling caterpillar. I'm impatient in wanting to develop into the person that I want to be.

Feeling nice and relaxed, I have a salad for dinner. I can't face a meat dish right now. Shortly afterward I head to bed for an early night's rest, and to reflect on the day's events. I wake up remembering that when I was a little girl, I used to enjoy playing dress-up. Wearing fake pearls and lace gloves was fun. I would spend hours trying on clothes that my mother had jammed into the little closet that she shared with my father. I remember being thrilled if I could find an outfit with some designer name attached to it, or pieces that matched. I tried to avoid the yelling that existed in my home so the closet became a safe place to hide, escape and get lost in my own thoughts. Pretending to be someone that I wasn't, but wanted to be, was my way of life. Drifting out of my nostalgic daydream, I decide that creating a garment with a decorative colorful outer shell will inspire the inner beauty that's within me.

This time I fancy something more grown up and revealing. My bedroom is filled with thrift store finds and bargains that were on clearance. I reach into the black section of my closet. Black is a color that no woman can live without. That will be the canvas on which to work. Taking sharp dagger scissors in hand, I masterfully cut a plunging neckline in a baggy dress that I have. I no longer want to be the girl who wears clothing that could be fooled as a tent. I grab some gold buttons and matching sequins out of my sewing kit that hasn't been used in years. I think it was given to me by my Aunt Jean when I was engaged to be married. I add a colorful belt taken from my best friend's bridesmaid dress, that is still hanging in the closet. Within an hour my creative masterpiece is done and it's time for the final reveal. Standing in front of the closet mirror, I think I've passed the episode of "What not to Wear." I'm proud of my creativity, but am I daring enough to wear it? I think I need a further boost of confidence.

The phone rings while I'm in my zone singing along to Journey's "Don't Stop Believin'" which is playing on the radio. Now for the real change from the old me. This song just takes me away. Another escape from what I'm dealing with in life. The phone keeps ringing. I answer, somewhat distracted.

"Hello Darling, it's me your fave, Guy!"

With a deep grin, I forget the lyrics of the song and know that this is a sign that change must happen.

"Hi Guy! How's it going?"

"I'm doing great! Thanks for asking. And you?"

"I'm OK. I have a favor to ask and you're gonna love it! What are you doing right now?"

I know that Guy will drop anything for me if I really ask. He's the kind of person that you can cry your blues to if your cat just died. He always has a strong shoulder to offer me comfort and support. We are tighter than Grandma's panties.

"Well, I was thinking of going by the local shoe store to get a pair of must have soft burnished leather shoes, but that can always wait. I'm very tempted by the plain lace up in black or cognac. But maybe my Prince Charming will help pay towards the price tag during the weekend. What do you have in mind Darling?" he asks.

"You are the exact person I need to help me out and create my new look!" I exclaim, pacing around my bedroom and glancing at my reflection in the mirror.

He coos, "Oh Darling, I've been waiting a lifetime to hear those words! I have so much I want to do with you. Meet me at the salon in twenty minutes. I will be there with scissors in hand to create a masterpiece for you."

"Got that. You're a doll! See you soon!"

I excitedly hang up the phone, quickly make myself up, and put on my newly created colorful stylish black dress. Keys in hand I head for the door. There's no stopping me now!

By the time I arrive at the salon, Guy is already there and waiting to greet me.

"Oh Darling! You have that look like your cherry has just been popped! I'm ready to make magic with you."

"I'm so excited. I can't wait to see what you can do for me!" I reply.

I take a seat and let the master take control. Twelve inches of hair fall to the ground. There is no turning back now.

There are no tears as I say goodbye to my graying, natural level seven dark blonde hair, and to the old me. Guy uses blonding crème to wash away my dullness and give me a vibrant new color. Doing balayage highlights, he hand paints the highlights in a sweeping motion moving from the base to the tip of the hair. At the base, he applies the color very lightly, while at the tip, the color is very heavy. The end result is chunky highlights that look naturally sun-bleached. It is pure magic as he turns the chair round so that he can greet the new me, mirror in hand. The modern blonde straight pixie hair with a jagged cut makes my blue eyes stand out. I look like a punk Blondie with distinctive photogenic features and two-tone bleach blonde hair. I could be her twin and sing "Heart of Glass" if I had some red lipstick on.

"Oh Guy! I love it!"

I start crying and hug him. Staring at the mirror I rhetorically ask, "Who is this person?"

He winks at me in approval.

"You look damn sexy girl! Now go out and conquer the world, and let me live vicariously through you for a change." I reach for my phone and take a selfie. I want to remember this transformational moment.

"Thank you so much Guy! You're the best!" I say with the biggest smile.

Heading towards the exit, like Alice preparing to go through the door into her exciting and unexplored new wonderland, I bump into Dawn Fry.

"Aww, don't you look adorable," she says, with one eye on me, and the other on her cash register.

She always seems to put her figures before employees. I'm not sure whether she's being sarcastic. I know from experience that she's always ready to make herself feel better by putting others subtly down.

It's funny, one minute she can be your best friend, like when her father was ill in hospital, the next minute, handing out disciplinary warnings like candy. Life is all about her and her self-absorbed ways. She has a tendency to lash out at others if she's having a bad day or relationship problems. Of course, she would always remind us that it was "Nothing personal, and strictly business at the end of the day." Her motives always seem to be based on making profits rather than friendships. Perhaps, that's how she survives in relationships, by keeping a distance to her heart and always having her walls up to those that surround her. I remind myself how thankful I am that I'm not related to her. This time she won't get the best of me, even though I always over analyze what she says, and what she really means.

"Thanks!" I say with conviction.

"I couldn't do what you have done. It's so daring and unlike you!"

I do not allow her backhanded compliment to get to me. Guy has done what Guy does best, which is to make me feel special, and to fill me with positive energy and self-confidence.

"See ya!" I reply to Dawn. "Wouldn't wanna be ya!" I think to myself, as I reach the door.

After leaving the salon I check my phone and notice a Facebook friend has contacted me. It's Pete Valaquez. I'm not boring! He friended me! I've won the popularity lottery contest, being voted the girl he admires. I see he's responded and sent me a message, "I happen to be thirty miles away from Newport visiting old friends. If you are around I would love to catch up."

Ordinarily, I would think about my answer for a week and consider the kid's soccer activities and band practice schedule. But since I have no kids to run around after, and nothing else to do right now, I type in my phone number and immediately respond, "Why not sooner rather than later?" I love how technology has made communicating with others so quick and easy.

A surge of adrenaline rushes through me as I get caught up in the moment.

I'm giddy with excitement that my new sense of confidence is causing me to be so impulsive, and wonder whether my eager response will be reciprocated.

I don't have to wait long to find out. Within minutes the phone rings.

"Hello, this is a blast from the past! Is that Sammie?" he inquires.

Like a schoolgirl on a first date, I get butterflies in my stomach.

"Why, yes it is! Petie is that you?" I ask.

"Sure is, but I go by Pete these days."

His deep voice has me immediately hooked. My mind races to his contagious laughter and the connections we had. I remember that he would teach me Spanish phrases, and I would repeat them diligently until I had mastered the delivery and pronunciation, such as "El burro sabe mas que tu," "eres muy feo," or "callate, tu estupido elefante." It was only afterward that I would find out that I had naively and unwittingly learned some new insult. We would roar with laughter for hours. We felt very comfortable and at ease with each other, and had stimulating conversations. He aroused me sexually and intellectually. He was insanely sexy with his mannerisms and charisma. I could gaze at him for hours, but my fantasies for him were never approached or realized. Pete says, "I know this is a long shot, but I'm going to a Latin Club tonight. A friend of mine is playing in the band. If you are around, you could join me."

It didn't take me long to give a quick, "Yeah I'm in." I make a note of the location of the club, and arrange to meet him in there.

My inner arousal points are beating like a schoolgirl. I'm in and determined to score. I can't contain my glee and anticipation. I make a point of purposefully stopping at a store which has a big sale on, where I splurge on pretty colored tops, a few pairs of pants, a couple of lace bras and some sexy panties, before heading for home to freshen up and get ready for my evening out. As I make myself up, I gaze in the bedroom mirror and can barely believe my transformation and that the beautiful stranger staring back at me is me.

My body heat has already risen as I enter the dark club where fast rhythmic music is playing. I realize that I don't even know what Pete looks like now, let alone my being able to spot him in this smoky room filled with sweating bodies dancing cheek to cheek to Latino beats. I look around and there he is, I think! A tall handsome well-dressed man with an irresistible smile. His goatee and random gray hairs are a welcome addition to his visual appeal. I can see he doesn't recognize me as his head tilts and his green eyes widen to meet my baby blues.

"Pete! It's me, Sammie!"

I give him a big hug like thirty years hasn't passed since we last met.

"Wow! I can't say that you haven't changed a bit, because I didn't recognize you," he says, as his eyes give the stamp of approval that my look is damn hot and sexy all rolled into one.

My shoulders rise to the occasion and I can feel a new diet taking over me. It's now the "I am in love with myself diet." Putting me first is on top of my list. I spoil myself with the pleasures of subjecting myself to the new me and indulge some more. I'm no longer perceived as a pathetic, frumpy mother of two. My life is taking on a new direction and meaning. Now a new dynamic woman has emerged and is ready to begin the next part of life's journey.

"Let's go right to where the action is!" he suggests.

He grabs my hand and whisks me to the dance floor. I remember dancing to Salsa music in my living room with Maria on occasion after we had made a meal and drank some wine. However, this is the real thing. After spending countless lonely Monday nights watching numerous reality dance shows, I can see they are doing the Bachata.

Pete's moves are intoxicating and I find myself in a trance watching his hips sway back and forth. The faster music adds to the rhythm of his footwork. He has playful twists and turns as he moves his hips in freestyle motion to the music. His foot moves to the outside, lifting up just before the first beat. Step, together, step, tap.

First, we concentrate on the open position, with our hands firmly together as the only means of contact. Our arms are loose and relaxed and palms facing up, palm on palm. The back of his masculine hand faces out and directs the moves. Elbows are bent at our sides as we move to the beat. Pete has the space and flexibility to do advanced turns and wiggle his alluring hips. I study his moves like a cat on the prowl. Immediately, I feel the music and find it easy to get the beat. Raising my right foot off the ground slightly, I'm forced to jut my hips out to the right. His hip lowers to the right side and appears to move higher. I follow his lead and let my body slowly melt next to his.

Our dancing alternates between the open, and more daringly to the close, romantic position. He has a slight bounce and moves his body up with the beat of the music. In the closed position our bodies are more intimate. Pete's arm is draped across my back with slight-to-strong contact between our bodies. The floor space is filling as we move closer and closer to each other. Pete uses his leading arm to hold my other hand out to the side. As we dance, Pete uses his outstretched hand to lead me gently, guiding my upper body towards his inviting direction. He does his turns to the time of the music.

He gives me his sexy eyes throughout our dance. They never leave my face or my side, as we move up and down to the beat, in synchronization with each other. I wiggle my hips closer to his, our whole bodies in constant motion, changing direction with every beat, as we glide together. The rhythm of the Bachata has us flowing together. This sensual dance has me moving in directions that I never knew were possible. My hips are more exaggerated than his, as I seductively move to the rhythm. He leads and I follow the direction of his motion, stepping to the right first, and then the left. He incorporates the back and forth motion as we become more reacquainted with our styles, molding into one.

He gets more complex and dazzling with some heel steps, leg crosses and twisting. Our shoulders are moving with the music and it feels so good. I step back as Pete steps forward. Our arms are in pumping motion and ready for action. The sweat from my body runs down my sexy black dress. Pete bends his knees and pops his hip for a low, sensual swaying motion. The pace is fast and my heart beats even faster. I move with soft hip movements and then a small pop of the hip like I've practiced with Maria in my living room. This time, I feel young and alive doing these maneuvers on the dance floor, with this handsome man. We have the same left four beats, right four beats. I step forward three beats and pop my hips on beat four, then step backward three beats and pop my hips again on the fourth beat. Moving my hips in the way I want my body to move next, I stare directly into his green eyes. He slides and does a flashy turn, to turn it up, as his feet are moving constantly. Our repetitive dance motion is like washing our hair together, lather, rinse and repeat. The actions are a whole body activity. In no time we are at one with our beats.

Soon, it's not only our hearts that are beating as one. Our lips meet and our tongues play along with the music. Deeply thrusting into each other mouths, I start to nibble his bottom lip and feel his manhood becoming aroused as our bodies brush against each other. I can tell by the way he uses his tongue that he would make an excellent candidate for oral. His tongue moves rapidly. I know in an instant that's where I want him to be, between my legs and licking my pink wet pussy. He's in control and I love it. His dominant hands hold me tight and for a moment I forget that we are still in a public place.

Hurriedly, we leave the dance-floor, past the bar, and into an empty handicapped bathroom stall. Locking the door with one hand, he grabs my breast with the other. Wildly, I gaze my seductive eyes at him in acceptance, that this will be the night that will break me free. I lift up my dress and drop my new panties to the floor unveiling my willing pussy.

Succumbing to his powers, he thrusts me against the sink and spreads my legs open and hitches my leg up. It feels so damn good to have a man want me so much. This is what I've been longing for, for a very long time. I want him so damn hard inside me. He responds with his erect cock. He fingers my pussy and twists the tips of my nipple. He curls his hips over mine and makes a bold move. I groan in sweet pleasure. He plunges his firm cock deep inside me. Deeper and deeper he moves. It feels like nothing I've ever felt before. His hips move back and forth, pushing hard, and my body glistens from his sweet scent.

Oh shit! This is good! Intense pleasures and burning desires fill me. I gasp as he thrusts faster and deeper. He groans and I know that I've made his desires come true too. My body is quivering. He kisses and sucks my neck. I lift my dress over my head to give him more visual sensations of my sexy lace bra and breasts. I can see his clenched butt in the mirror and it makes me even more wild and excited to feel his oncoming orgasm. Ooh, I can't catch my breath as the rhythm of his cock slides in and out of me. He slams his cock deep inside me. It hurts a little, but feels so good. I cry out in delight. My mind is blown and I press my nails into his back, marking my territory in this moment of passion. Before he orgasms I sink to the floor and he moves his firm cock between my breasts. I'm such a dirty girl and want to feel the intensity of his hot cum. I rub his cock hard and he explodes on my tits.

Ahh, such a sweet sensation. I close my eyes and know that I am a sensual woman.

~ Recipe 4 ~
The Confidence Of Extreme Indulgence

Prep time:	Two days
Serves:	Many

This recipe is designed to be a show-stopper. A few simple indulgences will add zest for new dimensions. I will not be afraid to go to extremes and make the ultimate sacrifice for this experience. In fact, finding myself while being impulsive is the confidence I need to succeed. Radiant passion, conviction and strength are all the ingredients that are sandwiched together. If the fake-ass confidence is left at the door, finding myself will not be lost in this recipe.

Creativity:	Body art
Cost:	Go topless
Culinary:	Drink cocktails
Culture:	Fly
Connect:	Leave a tip

A deep sense of contentment has come over my body. I wake up in the arms of this sexy man in his hotel room and now I feel popular. I've really scored "a big one." I want to scream, "Look what I got in my bed!" My mates would never believe that I could have such a prize. His cock was incredibly big and gave me such an orgasm, I would say. I would tell everyone that I've never felt such a big cock giving me pleasure over and over again. Or maybe I'm starting to think like a guy. Am I trying to compensate for my own inadequacy or am I trying to make my friends jealous?

I heard about a report from some sex survey that men think about sex about every half an hour, while women tend to think of it just once a day. If men are thinking about sex so frequently, how do they get any work done? Maybe with finding myself, my sexuality has awoken itself and is now on overdrive. I'm making up for lost time.

Pete rolls over and kisses my breasts, "Good morning sexy!"

He gazes into my eyes and I'm lost. I wrap my arms around his bare chest and cannot think of any other responsibilities I have in life.

"Are you doing anything for the next few days?" he whispers, "I don't want this to end."

End? How could I possibly think of ending this, when this amazing feeling has just taken over? I'm in a trance or some sort of spell and his name is Pete. At this moment I would do anything that this man asks. I'm a lemming and I will follow him. He could say jump and I will jump in his direction. He has control and a strong sense of dominance over me and I'm helpless.

"What do you have in mind?"

I look at him like a young puppy hoping to be adopted.

"Come fly with me. I have to go back to New Orleans tonight."

Before I can even process his request I respond, "Yes! Yes, I will go with you."

His talkative eyes sparkle as he gives me more kisses along my neck. I get down on my knees and begin pleasuring his awesomely large cock. Discovering what it means to give some really good head, I wrap my lips around his cock, and rhythmically move it in and out of my mouth, while holding the base of his penis firmly between my thumb and forefinger. I know that he's enjoying it because he moans with delight. My tongue is rapid and licks up and down his penis. I definitely did not learn this in my long failed marriage. My ex's penis could be featured in an erectile dysfunction commercial. There was not much action in the bedroom or between the sheets. I lost out a lot in married life because of our limited sex life.

My primal instincts take over and although I've never done so before, I feel an urge to taste his sweet cum in my mouth. I look up into his eyes and know that I'm pleasing him. The thought of pleasuring him orally to orgasm gets my pussy all wet and tingly. If I were to take a snapshot of his face when he cums it might look like he's just stepped on a nail, his jaw elongated like he's singing in the boys' choir at Christmas. I know he has a present for me and I can't resist tasting my special Christmas package. I take him in my mouth again, deeper and deeper. My other hand is gently massaging his balls, until I feel his muscles tense up, as he groans in ecstasy before exploding and rewarding me with his orgasm.

At the last moment I chicken out and withdraw my mouth from his cock, watching as his hot cum shoots towards me, landing on my face and trickling down my cheek. I giggle to myself and think this is the cheapest fucking facial I've ever been given, and that the girls at work would be so jealous. I'm savoring each moment I have with this man. The passion of pleasing him leaves me satisfied. We clean up, get dressed and I arrange to meet him at the airline ticket counter in Providence later in the afternoon.

I drive home in order to gather a few things in a travel bag to run away with him, my mind racing with possibilities. I cannot believe that my lifestyle has changed so profoundly in only a few days. I go to the ATM and grab a fair share of cash, because I've no idea what I might encounter and I want to be prepared. I'm ready to take on the "good life."

Spontaneity is running my life and I'm going with the flow. It's a long time since I've done something that didn't require any pre-planning or preparation. This is new territory for me. I surprise myself by being so impulsive.

Any fears I have disappear when I see his beaming face at the airport.

"Hello gorgeous!"

He greets me with a warm smile and a kiss. Not just a kiss on the cheek, like you do when you are friendly. A real kiss, like he wants me. I melt with satisfaction and my heart skips a beat. I swear, with his reassuring comments, he's taking years off my life. I feel like my hot air balloon has been filled and is ready to take off.

We present our identification at the check-in. Pete receives, smiles, and hands me my boarding pass.

"I thought I would surprise you sweetheart."

Did he just call me sweetheart? I'm not used to a man being so generous with his affections. After feeling like I was not previously worthy of such gifts, I'm basking in the gift of compliments that he continues to shower me with. It's nice to feel appreciated and wanted.

I look down at my boarding pass when we reach the security checkpoint and I see my name Samantha Fleming seat 2A. I look at it like Willie Wonka has just given me a golden ticket. This kind of indulgence is something foreign to me. Never in a million years could I afford to splurge on such luxuries. First class is only for someone with deep pockets or the business traveler with a generous employer.

"Is this what I think it is?" I ask, giddy with excitement. I've never ever flown first class before.

"Yes darling, and it's all for you," he replies.

I'm in awe of him.

"I love it!"

I give him the biggest kiss and hug ever. I feel like royalty. My heart is happy and I'm savoring the moments. We take our seats in the first class area of the plane and are greeted by a member of the cabin crew. We are provided with a complimentary glass of wine. The leather seats are large, comfortable and spacious.

This is the first time in my life that I've ever felt so highly valued.

"I hope you like the luxuries of first class because you deserve this special kind of treatment, Baby!" he says, taking my hand.

I nod eagerly.

"Yes, Pete. A girl could get used to this kind of treatment."

He tilts his head and gazes into my eyes.

"Baby, you make it so easy."

I smile and blush, "This is good, almost too good to be true. You really have done well for yourself. Funny how life happens."

The plane begins to take off after the flight attendant has gone through her safety demonstrations. After we reach our flying altitude, the flight attendant brings us more wine, which now has me feeling utterly relaxed and comfortable. Pete is my own personal masseur as he gently rubs my shoulders and caresses my arm. I feel like a princess going on a romantic voyage with my lover for the weekend.

"Pete, Do you remember dancing to the YMCA at Greg's Halloween party?" I ask with a giggle.

"Oh yes. How could I forget that one! I was dressed in a Cowboy outfit and I think you were dressed as a Native American Indian, with your hair in pigtails."

We spontaneously sing the chorus and do the arm actions. It seems so natural and such fun.

He chuckles while he reminisces.

The flight attendant playful nods at him and smiles, as I'm sure she has her own pleasant memories of the song. Who could not, as it has always been such a big party hit? I laugh.

"I can't believe you remembered that!"

"Baby, I could never forget your deserving smile and those cute moves." Pete says.

"Really? You do know how to touch a girl's heart. How about the time a group of us went out after the football game for pizza. We got kicked out because we were too noisy."

"Yeah, I remember that. I tried to follow you home and get a ride with you. But you quickly vanished before I could catch up."

His eyes are alight with fond memories. I bite my lower lip and clench my teeth. Damn it, if I could turn back time. I would have been more adventurous and maybe looked out for my Petie. Who knows where fate would have brought us in the current time.

Pete notices my startled look and surprises me by taking control of my disappointment. He reads my mind like an open book. He grabs my hand and slides it against his firm cock, without anyone noticing. He's so sly and quick with his smooth moves.

His bold gesture quickly arouses my pussy.

He whispers in my ear, like a teasing, playful sexy man.

"How would Baby like to join the Mile high club with me someday? I'm sure we could arrange something in your future."

I'm immediately distracted from all my previous thoughts and now focused on his seductive charms.

I lick my lips, "I like what you are offering and I could easily get used to more with you."

"Good! Hold on tight because more is what you will get with me Baby."

He winks at me and holds my hand tightly in his.

The service provided is second to none. The airline's little touches haven't been lost on me like the warm nuts and glassware for my drink.

The plane lands in Detroit, where we have to almost run through the airport to make our connecting flight to Louis Armstrong. Several more hours flying first class, some more wine, and I'm ready for anything. Arriving at the airport, smiling ladies from the visitor's bureau greet us with purple, green and gold beads to wear around our necks. The free and overflowing beads sets the tone of a genuine relaxed atmosphere.

A cab ride later and we arrive in New Orleans. We are immediately met with the embrace of the historic charm and warm friendly ambassadors that greet us. Jazz music fills my ears and like BB King would sing, I'm ready to "Let the Good Times Roll." I wonder what life would be like if I lived here.

The Big Easy should be called "The Happy Place" because happiness surrounds the city. It greets you from every angle. Pete looks determined to further please me. We arrive at his condo in the Warehouse District. I immediately figure out that he loves the lifestyle of the city and has surrounded himself in luxury. I'm impressed but baffled as to how this man has become so successful.

Within half an hour passion takes over and I find myself on my back, naked. I'm beyond aroused and feeling multiple orgasms, all due to the spell that Pete has cast over me. I cannot remember a day that I've experienced so many orgasms, and we haven't even had the main course yet. His fingers explore and press all my points and he takes his time in getting to know them. He reads my body like a book, and when he hits one of my spots, he explores it in greater detail, leading my pussy to heightened sensitivity and even more explosive orgasms. It's such a turn on, how he finger fucks me to the point where my juices are dripping with intense heat.

Whether it's my clitoris or my vagina, he pleasures it and makes each region accountable for producing further heirs to his kingdom of climaxes. Pete is the king when it comes to giving me orgasms. This is new territory that I've never encountered before.

I lay on his king-size bed, caressed by the soft touch of its silk sheets, legs apart, moaning and groaning in sheer bliss. I no longer know myself or the world around me. This experience transcends me and is changing my perspective on sex. The intensity is beyond mind blowing. At this very moment, all I'm aware of are these sensations and pleasurable feelings. Overwhelming feelings of passion encompass me. Trembling in excitement to the new God of sex, and master of my found sexuality, I'm at his mercy as he sticks his hard cock deep inside me. Nothing else matters right now but these euphoric feelings of pleasure and bliss.

He lifts my legs up, resting them on his shoulders, pins my arms down by holding onto my wrists, and thrusts himself hard and deep inside my hot wet pussy. My pussy is so hungry for his firm red cock. His movements remind me of his dancing, the way he moves and thrusts his hips rhythmically in and out of me, sometimes teasing me with slow moves, before thrusting harder and deeper and faster. I gasp for breath as our passion heats up the room and my body temperature rises with the thrill of our love-making. He moves to the missionary position, putting his hands underneath my ass, and starts grinding slow and deep, his hips moving in a circular motion. I sense that he's ready to cum and I want to feel every drop of it, deep inside me.

"Oh Pete, you are the best! I want to feel you! Ooh, cum inside me! Fill me up!"

Pete's body jerks and tenses, and then he cries out "Ahh" and dutifully complies, shooting his load into me. The warmth of his cum feels so good inside me. I'm complete and satisfied.

I grab a towel to wipe myself, and then we kiss and cuddle. I rest my head on his chest and in my post-orgasmic afterglow I fall asleep in his arms.

The following morning I awaken to the rich aroma of dark roasted coffee.

"Hey Baby, I brought you this," he says, putting down a cup of café latte on the bedside table.

He kisses my forehead and gives me his charming smile.

"Just what I need," I purr.

"Sweetheart, you ain't seen nothing yet! I have some plans for us today. We will head to the French Quarter in an hour."

He talks with a firm manner and sexy voice. I feel like I'm falling deeper and deeper under his spell.

Holy shit! This man really knows how to take control and dominate. I'm at his beck and call and I will do anything he asks. He has me acting so out of character.

I quickly energize myself in the shower, and dress, putting on a plunging red top and clinging black pants. Underneath I wear my sexy black lace bra and fresh panties, which further adds to my confidence levels. To finish off my hot new look I put on high heels, a warm jacket and red lipstick. As I start to bloom into a sexually active woman, I want to forget about the baggy dresses and fashion disaster clothing that could have been mistaken as curtains.

Before I wake up from this fantasy life, I'm ready to go out and explore.

The smell of caramelized pralines and sounds of laughter fill the air. Tourist and voodoo shops sprinkle the streets. We head to a jazz pub on Bourbon Street and Pete welcomes me to his hometown by ordering a Hurricane, which is one of the quintessential New Orleans cocktails. It has sweet fruity taste with a rum kick, which has me smiling. We toast to a new meaning in life.

"Here is another you must try," he says, handing me a Sazerac.

It is so delicious! I understand why it's America's first cocktail, and it's a classic. My cheeks feel warm and jazz music fills my ears. I feel happy and relaxed. Despite the unfamiliar surroundings, I feel comfortable in this new territory. I start to move and groove to the music, while involuntarily tapping my foot to the beat. The musical gumbo is a sweet mix of all the things that feel right about this city. We have a few more drinks and life is feeling real good. I look across the room and notice a beautiful woman, eyelashes perfectly curled, long straight blonde hair, wearing a tight fitting pink dress. She's the kind of girl that you can't help but notice.

Pete spots that I have been distracted.

"Why the funny look, sexy?" he asks curiously, winking at me, and awaiting my response.

"You caught me," I reply. "I was looking at that hot woman over there."

"Don't worry. He has more junk than you'll ever have. Pretty boy that one!" he responds in amusement.

I feel silly and pathetic. I laugh and blush with embarrassment.

Lou Reed's "Walk on the Wild Side" comes to mind. I can almost hear the saxophone blasting away in that song as we sit there.

The drink continues to flow and the hours pass by while we listen to musical jazz rhythms, people-watch and soak in the atmosphere.

"What is that tattoo?" I ask Pete, pointing to the picture on his right upper arm.

I'm sure I've seen that symbol somewhere before, but right now I can't place it.

"It's called a Fleur-de-lis, and it signifies perfection, light and life," he tells me.

He's enjoying my playfulness and he stares me right in the eye and says, "How would you like to join my team?"

"Sure, whatcha have in mind?" I ask.

"Let's share tattoos!" he says.

It sounds sexy and something I know my dad wouldn't approve. But my midlife habits aren't going to stop me. I would do anything Pete demands of me at this point. I'm beyond my limits and under his control.

Before I have time to think it over, we leave the music filled dimly lit room, and head to a nearby tattoo shop.

Inside, the walls are covered with pictures and drawings, mostly colored, others just plain black templates. So many different designs! Birds, flowers, flags, dragons, cartoon characters. I giggle as the visuals remind me of the books I used to color in as a child.

There are a number of catalogs on the brightly lit glass display cabinets in the store, each holding numerous different images and styles.

I am introduced to Gary. He has a well-built frame, wears a Harley t-shirt, and faded blue jeans. His arms are almost completely covered in tattoos, which to me looks like a tapestry of foreign artwork.

"Hi. How can I help you today?" he asks.

"Do you have any Fleur-de-lis designs?" I bravely reply.

"Sure," he says, and reaches for one of the books which is prominently displayed on the front shelf.

He flicks through the pages, until he comes to a stop at a page with half a dozen different design interpretations.

"I think we already have an idea of which one we want," Pete says, signaling to Gary with a thumbs up sign.

One of them catches my eye almost immediately.

"I like that one!"

Pete nods in approval, and a fee is agreed for the work, which Gary suggests will take around an hour.

"You be alright here Sammie?" Pete asks. "I've some business that needs attending to. I'm going to pop out for a while and leave you to it. I will be back before you're through."

He gives me a hug and a kiss and leaves me with Gary. He leads me into a side-room and gestures that I should relax on the black faux leather reclining chair which is positioned in the center of the small room.

"I will need to make a stencil of your design. Give me a couple of minutes," he says and leaves the room.

I look around and see more tattoo images stuck to the walls, it's like a miniature art gallery or a school classroom decorated with children's pictures. Very creative and colorful. The chair is like the kind you would find in a dentist's office and is really comfortable to sit on. To my right there is a swivel chair on wheels, with armrests, and to its left is a chest of drawers with a tattoo machine, and other equipment on top of it.

He walks back in holding a carbon paper Fleur-de-lis stencil and closes the door quietly behind him.

"Now that I have the design you want, where would you like me to ink it for you?" he asks.

"I think, maybe here," I say, and slightly embarrassed I point to area above my right breast.

"No problem," he says, matter of fact. "You will need to remove your top though. We don't want to get blood or ink on your clothing."

The alcohol running through my system appears to have lowered my inhibitions because I remove my top and bra without too much thought. I figure that, like a doctor, he will be used to seeing flesh, and will view mine only as business as usual, rather than as a sexual object. I don't have any control over my nipples becoming aroused though. He adjusts the position of the chair, so that I am at the perfect angle for him to work on. He puts on latex gloves, wipes my upper right breast with alcohol, then takes out a small razor and shaves the area to be tattooed. His hands are more comfortable with my breast than I am. He wipes again and then carefully positions the carbon paper. After its removal it leaves a stencil Fleur-de-lis outline on my breast. He reaches into the top drawer and takes out a sterile needle and fits it onto the tattoo machine, preparing his equipment like a methodical doctor. He then reaches back into the drawer, bringing out a small plastic bottle filled with black ink.

"OK, are you ready for this?" he asks.

I smile and nod. I'm a little apprehensive as to the needle, and the degree of pain it will inflict. It reminds me of when as a child the dentist needed to give me a filling which required sticking a needle into my gums to numb the impending pain. The fear of the needle was usually worse than the reality.

He tells me relax and stay still, and then after dipping his needle into the ink bottle, begins his work of drawing the artwork onto me. He uses his left hand to hold his canvas steady, and with the tattoo machine in his right hand, he converts my temporary body-stencil into a permanent feature.

Despite being anxious and tensed up, the needle doesn't hurt half as much as I expect. The sensation is a tolerable mix of stinging and burning.

His face is in my personal space and I can't help but notice him and how intently focused he is on his work. I watch in fascination and curiosity as he meticulously and systematically works his way around the design outline, frequently having to wipe away excess ink and blood. He tries to make small conversation to relax me each time he wipes.

I see my skin beginning to redden around the tattooed area as blood rushes to the surface, to fight this foreign invasion. I glimpse the black inked outline, which is quickly becoming a familiar shape, as he reaches for more ink. Within a quarter hour or so the outline is complete, and he passes me a hand mirror so that I can see the work he's done so far.

"I am impressed!"

Despite my bloodied stinging tender breast, the shape and style of the outline is perfectly drawn and positioned.

"What colors would you like?" he asks, opening the middle drawer to reveal a collection of bottles of vibrant colored inks that would excite any artist.

I select two colors from his vast array, and he begins the process of coloring and shading.

He puts the colors together like a puzzle, filling in the pattern in fine detail.

I start to grimace at each painstaking stroke.

Damn! This is beginning to hurt! Sometimes it feels like a razor blade being scrapped over a bad sunburn. This painful discomfort causes me to clench my teeth as I try not to let out a scream.

I try to distract my mind from the pain by looking at his generous tattoos. I notice and ask him about the dream catcher on his left arm. He stops his work momentarily, lifts his gaze towards me, and tells me that it symbolizes the life that was lost. His late son, Alan, had died in a terrible accident at a young age.

"The world we live in cannot be perfect and my son will always have his dreams upon me. I carry his spirit wherever I go and with whoever I touch," Gary says.

In deep reflection, I think about how intimate I feel with this stranger and how his pain lingers within his heart and it touches mine. He feels extremely close, both in proximity and connection.

I no longer feel the pain of the tattoo process, as I gain a sense of affinity.

He wipes the blood and excess ink gently off my breast.

"OK. I think we are nearly finished."

He passes me the mirror. Marveling at Gary's talent and artistry, I gaze at the black with hint of antique gold and purple Fleur-de-lis tattoo. The definition is not complete, but I know this imprint will last forever.

At that moment there is a knock at the door and Pete is standing there.

"Am I OK to come in?" he asks, noticing my state of undress.

"Sure!" I reply proudly.

He walks into the room and with a big grin on his face looks in admiration at my new tattoo.

"Nice artwork Gary!" he says.

"Thanks a lot!"

Gary finishes his work by sterilizing the tattooed area once more by rubbing anti-bacterial ointment onto it. He then takes some plastic wrap and tapes it over the area, explaining to me what I need to do in order to look after it. I carefully put my top back on.

I thank Gary, give him a tip, and we leave.

Pete whispers in my ear, "Don't worry Baby, I will make that breast feel so much better, later."

He gives me a deep kiss and I forget the pain that I'm feeling. It really hurts and I wonder if, like childbirth, I would do it again once I see the image in the flesh.

Wearing my new badge of honor, I avoid putting on my black bra, instead stuffing it into my jacket pocket. The petals of the Fleur-de-lis are like the Holy Trinity but right now I don't feel very holy.

Pete kisses me deep and hard with his luscious tongue.

"There is more where that came from hot stuff," he says.

We head back to Bourbon Street near a strip joint in the heart and soul of New Orleans. A few more drinks and I can't remember the time, or if I'm walking straight. Dodging the puddles in the street, I'm not sure if they are caused by the rain or from spilled drinks. Each bar we pass plays a different tune, each band seeming louder than the last. We head to a dimly lit bar with neon lights. I see a young red-haired bartender who appears to know Pete. She greets him with a smile, hugs and kisses. He looks my way, gives her a nod, and she walks over to me and takes my arm. I feel like I've been accepted on the kickball team at school.

"Reddy Head" guides me up a flight of stairs and says, "You will see the best views from the balcony."

She has loads of colorful beads in her hands and looks ready to party.

Music fills the street, which is full of fun-loving partygoers. Some are standing around drinking, others are waving their hands in the air, many are dancing with their eyes fixated on the balcony. People are clapping and having a good time. Young men are walking past and one small group yells, "Show us your tits!"

Reddy lifts up her shirt, baring her pert breasts, to cheers and whistles of some of the young men.

She looks at me with a mischievous smile, plants a kiss on my lips and says, "Come on girl. Show them your stuff!"

Frightened, I gaze at the crowd below. I feel an impressive sense of commanding attention. I wonder if this is how Eva Peron felt when she went onto the balcony to address her nation, although showing her "stuff" would definitely not have been on her agenda. I'm elevated above the crowd, which looks up to me for an immediate response. Getting caught up in the impulsive moment, I turn to Reddy with a playful look. I laugh but eagerly want to join in on the fun. I feel like I've been accepted by this enchanting woman.

Another group of young men walk by and they are holding handfuls of gold and purple beads. Getting caught up with the rush of adrenaline, I lift up my red top to flash my boobs at the crowd. I feel the thrill of showing my stuff to a group of happy, drunk onlookers. The crowd claps and screams in delight. I forget all about the tattoo that I've covered. The men cheer and throw some beads my way. As I try to catch the beads, I see Reddy out of the corner of my eye. She moves in front of me and looks astonished.

"I didn't know that I was too late."

Her voice is firm and my heart sinks.

"Too late for what?" I stutter.

"How deep are you into this?" Reddy says, staring at me.

"What are you talking about? I was just getting into the fun of this. Did I do something wrong?"

I squirm and start to fluster.

She takes me back into the building towards a dimly lit corridor and sits me down.

"You look like you don't get it. Sure you are pretty, but what's your story? You have a Saint on your breast, don't you? You don't want to join his team and be one of his Bitches!" she tells me, pointing to my breast.

I put my hand to the breast of my new tattoo. I wasn't even showing it. How did she know?

"I don't know what you are trying to say." I answer, confused.

Her face looks grim.

"Listen. I've seen it all before and you aren't the first. Pete marks his territory with the Saint. It's worse than a tramp stamp. That's what he does with all his women. You aren't his first conquest. He marks his territory and his women."

Tears fill my eyes and my jaw drops open. I can't believe that I've been taken for a ride. I'm too vulnerable and trusting.

"What do I do now?"

I feel anger for being played like a fool. I allowed myself to be caught up in this whole situation and forgot who I am and what I stand for. The pleasures that aroused me took over my sensibilities.

"Run! Run as fast as you can and don't look back. Here is a back door, don't come back here. It will only get worse."

She points to the door and pushes me towards it. I hear her but I can't process my thoughts properly. My fight or flight response has me feeling frozen and numb.

I went over my limits and didn't know when to stop. I must not surrender my views or myself. I want to get away and run as quickly as I can, but I realize that I can't. All my stuff is at Pete's condo and I'm too far from home.

With the best acting I've ever done in my life, I return to Pete, who is sitting with a beer, talking with a group of people at a table.

"Pete, this tattoo is really hurting. I need to get back to the condo and lie down, maybe sleep the pain off. Can you take me back?"

"No I can't take you Sam, I've business to attend to here. I don't know when I'll be finished. I'll call you a cab and give you the key-code to my apartment," and with that he takes out his phone, dials and speaks to someone and then says, "The cab is on its way. I will see you when I get back. Sleep well. I've plans for us tomorrow."

No hug, no kiss.

I head for the exit and wait for the cab to arrive. Arriving back at his condo, I gather my belongings together. I need to change my clothing and to clean my tattooed breast. The paper tape is already coming way from my skin due to the moisture and excess ink seeping out. I head for the bathroom to clean up. It's a messy job but I manage to very gently and carefully clean my tender skin. I wipe down and dry the plastic wrap, but the tape on it has lost its stickiness. In my search for more tape, opening one of the drawers I find some, together with a roll of dollars held together with an elastic band.

I stare at the roll for a moment, my heart beating harder and faster.

"Fuck you, Pete Valaquez!" I say out loud as I pick it up and put it in my purse.

I re-dress my tattoo and myself, and then call the cab firm, whose number is on the business card I picked up on my cab ride.

"To the airport please," and I'm out of here.

~ Recipe 5 ~
Going Beyond My Norms

Prep time:	Two to three days
Serves:	One

This recipe sets itself apart by going beyond the norms of what is acceptable. Breaking "out of the box" and finding out who can be trusted. How to use the ingredients is important in this recipe. Try not to load up on too much at one time. Don't be concerned with the perception of others.

Creativity:	Play with toys
Cost:	Quit job
Culinary:	Eat German food
Culture:	Go fast
Connect:	Gamble

I pick up the ringing phone.

"Hello?"

"Honey, I've been worried about you."

It's my dad. His voice wraps me up, like giving a warm blanket and chicken soup to a sick child. It welcomes and comforts me.

"Hi Daddy."

I wait for the expected silence. He can never make a conversation flow easily.

"Jason has called me because the kids wanted to talk to you. Josh and Jess got their report cards yesterday. They keep asking where you are."

In that instant I feel that I'm being scolded for my non-mommy like behavior.

Fear grabs me and brings my heart back to center.

"OK Daddy. I will call them."

"Honey, You can take it or leave it, but they are still your kids," he says sternly.

I realize that I have a responsibility, but right now I'm not fit to look after myself. I'm not a slave to my home life. I have nothing, and not even the lines in the mirror seem clear right now. I look at the piles of clothing in my house as I pace the halls with the phone. Uneasiness and discomfort fills my shoes.

"Dad, I hear you."

Guilt rushes over me again. Damn guilt!

"Yes, but are you really listening?"

I know that I'm not perfect. I did not pass the "perfect test," like my brother Adam. I rarely seem to please him or gain his approval, when what I really need is loving, authentic and genuinely welcoming arms. Instead, I get the opposite. I am who I am and he doesn't like it. We are never totally honest with each other. There are so many unspoken words. Words that should be said, but aren't. It makes for difficult conversation and communication, and sometimes cuts to my heart. It's not just this time. It goes back to childhood. I feel like I've always been the problem. I don't want him to blame me anymore for the way that my life has turned out, or for my failed marriage.

"I gotta go Dad. I'll be late for work. I'll speak to you later."

I know this is a lie but I can't take the pressure anymore.

My lecture is over for now.

There are times when I've felt like telling him how much I hate him for the way that he makes me feel about myself. Work isn't something I've focused on lately due to my indulgences. My mission and purpose has been to find and redefine my sense of self, and determine where I'm going and living.

Changing into blue jeans, high length leather boots and leopard print top, I notice a change in the mirror. I know it isn't my tired eyes becoming old and unfocused. I see a sense of direction. I can't yet say who I am, or what my purpose is. Maybe it's the newly found confidence that I feel within myself. I smile but I'm not engaged in my own smile. The stranger before me needs to unveil herself. I want to be accepted and not judged by my family and peers. Walking to the salon, I feel a sense of normalcy and belonging. Standing for long hours is commonplace with hairdressing. Tired aching feet and hands are the norm. I know that I can correct disastrous hair colors and make a cut just like the pictures show in the magazines. I've made women feel pretty again. I've shared my life with strangers who confide their darkest secrets to me. Many of my clients have become friends. At times, the salon is like high school with the amount of gossip that goes on between the busy bees. This week I may be the topic of conversation, due to my unscheduled absence, next week it will be someone else. Today's news is tomorrow's fish and chip paper. This time I know that I will be the "O.J. Simpson" of the group. I'm not one that turns to the boss whenever there is a problem. Everyone will be focusing on my crimes and will be watching me closely. Where is my attorney to say, "If the glove doesn't fit, you must acquit?" I need my own Johnny Cochran representing me, but all I have is my sole voice. As soon as I arrive, Dawn, my passive aggressive boss approaches me.

"Well look who it is! I thought you'd fallen off the face of the earth. There is something about that you that's different."

She's usually busy with her routine, filling out the inventory order or chatting with the customers. I wish someday she would be totally honest and say what she really thinks. I would love to give her a taste of her own medicine. If she experienced the world through someone else's eyes for just one day she may see the light. I've always pretended to like her but now she's about to find out the truth.

"Well, I kind of like the way I look and feel for that matter," I retort, sarcasm coating my voice.

The song by Phil Collins, "I Don't Care Anymore," comes to mind. I feel myself beginning to lose control. My emotions are in the spotlight and they are taking over my head. My mom's dramatic style and tone are taking over me. I remember how she would yell and scream when she was damn mad. Everyone would notice her when she spoke. The flashback of my mother gives me an uncontrollable urge that I've never felt before. I will survive and I have no fear in this moment.

"I think you have missed a few days of work already. How does that feel and look? Because from my point it won't look good on the unemployment line."

She gives me one of those cutesy smiles that she parades around all the time.

I hate her, not only because she's a skinny girl that never could fill a pair of jeans, or a bra for that matter, and not because she prances around in her high-heeled shoes like she was born with them. I hate her because she will say something negative, like you screwed up in your job, and then compliment you on the purple floral top you are wearing. The funny thing is, she will then try to make small talk, by saying purple is her favorite color, or she will say something like, "My New Year's resolution is to be better organized. Too bad that others don't share the same point of view."

Usually, if I don't immediately agree with her or do exactly as she says, I look like the bad guy. She only responds positively to yes-men, and has a condescending tone which she uses to teach you a lesson when you challenge her. She's the master at keeping score of who wins the battle, and won't let you live it down if you outsmart her. If only truth and honesty could guide her actions.

I get it. I can't live up to her standards. Like I really give a damn about phony people like her. You have to wonder where people like that get off with their backhanded compliments. How can they sleep at night with their cold-hearted ways?

She's pure ripe with a fresh smell of dingleberries. She's the master one, always up my ass. Did she go to the "Lame University" or something? A place designed to spit out bitches that only screw others to get to the top. She doesn't care who she hurts in the process to get there. Power, control and moving up are her only goal. She doesn't mind who she stomps on in the process. She wears a fake smile, behind which is a frown. An untold story littered with many moments of sadness. She can't even hold down a long-term relationship. I think that men have learned to stay away from a woman like her. She will grow old, lonely and desperate for a real life. Her true smile is never revealed to those around her. She hasn't realized that a true smile is a window to humanity. That's why she's the boss without a relationship. Her work will be the only relationship that will ever keep her, because real people are too smart for her own insecurities and drama. She uses that fake smile against me in ways I can't control.

No one likes getting yelled at and at this very moment I can either shut up and put up, or fight back and release the emotions that I'm feeling. Oh, fuck it!

"You know, I don't need you, or this place for that matter. I'm better than this!" I belt out.

I feel a rush of blood to my head and a huge surge of adrenaline. I can't hold back. I want what I want and I want it now, and this job isn't one of them. I'm on a runaway train and the momentum won't stop. I cannot be an expert in everything I do or touch. I will never live up to her crazy standards and ass kissing. This is something in my life I can't care about anymore. I will miss friends like Maria, Guy Rinker and his catty comments about the clients.

"Do you know what you are saying?" she asks, turning her head right at me.

"You know what? You can take this fucking job and shove it up your skinny ass! This is not where I want to be."

I can't win for losing and I'm tired of being the scapegoat. At this moment I'm just plain tired and I really don't give a fuck anymore. I've wanted to say these words to her for a very long time but I've never before had the courage to say them. What happens to someone who really says what they feel? What are the repercussions? How will it change my life? I guess I'm about to find out.

"Fine! You know where the door is. Don't let it hit you too hard on the way out!"

She rolls her eyes and gives me a blank stare. I know that will be the last time I'll see her and right now I'm not bothered. If I had the chance to do it all again, I know that in a heartbeat I wouldn't change my mind for anything. It's a life changer for me. I will no longer be attached to people who put me down like she does.

For the second time in a week, I walk away from controlling people. I set myself free from her chains. I exit the salon, smiling. I have to keep walking and not look back. I don't want to think about the implications or consequences of my actions right now. I did not plan to do this, it just happened this way. Of course, I had sometimes dreamed of what it would be like. This is not my normal behavior or how I would normally live my life. Somehow, I never imagined that this would be an option for me. For now, I'm free to do what I want. I've taken back control and no one can dictate on what I do from nine to five. I return to the confines of my home and try to pull myself together.

I reach up for a box hidden at the back of the closet, that has been gathering dust and has hardly been touched since after my bachelorette party. I'm ready for some real self-motivation techniques right now.

My friends gave me a Jack Rabbit vibrator as a joke present before I got married and tied down. The penis shape and clitoral stimulator were more pleasurable than my ex-husband ever was during our long, often sexless, marriage. I don't know why it still sits there, rarely used, on the top shelf. Is it because the values I was brought up with told me that it was naughty and taboo, or, is it because my faith tells me that masturbation is sinful?

I must have used it only a few times, probably after a couple of glasses of Chardonnay while on my own. I've never been totally comfortable exploring my body without consuming alcohol first.

Sure, it feels good, but I've never really given it the full attention and time that it deserves. Maybe I don't even give myself the attention that my needs demand either. God has given me hands and I've used them occasionally, but even then there was always the chance that one of the kids would walk into the bedroom, which was a real turn off. The house is empty, and I'm alone.

Taking the medium-sized rabbit out of its box, I fill it with new batteries.

I haven't masturbated in a long time or really taken the time to explore myself. Now, without distraction, I can be the master of my own domain.

Where is the shame in discovering and pleasuring myself? Stimulation with a battery-operated device has always seemed so foreign to me, but I surrender my anxious feelings for ones yearning for pleasure.

I turn the rabbit on and feel the vibrations running through it.

Laying on my back on the bed, I rest the vibrating head on my breast and move it slowly and gently around, enjoying the tingling sensations that it gives me. My nipples become erect with pleasure and excitement, my body gets goose bumps, and I'm getting a warm feeling in my panties. I close my eyes and hold it to my nipple for a moment enjoying the tingly feeling. My clit starts throbbing and I can feel myself getting warmer and wet.

I press one of the rubber buttons at the rabbit's base and the vibration changes into a strong rhythmic pulse. The pulse electrifies me as I move it lower and lower down my body, guiding it around, discovering areas of great sensitivity, and reveling in the feelings they elicit. My pussy is getting so wet. I have a strong urge and desire for my rabbit to meet my pussy.

I lift up my ass, pull off my panties and bend my knees towards the ceiling. I rub the rabbit in a circular motion on my clit and insert the dildo in and out of my honey pot. I close my eyes and feel each sensation. I let myself go as my moaning escalates to high pitches of pleasure. A song of moans and sexual melody ensues.

My body sweats as it moves and flushes with excitement.

"Oh my God!" I exclaim, panting and breathing hard.

I feel years younger as a boost of energy runs through my body. I start fingering myself and plunge my fingers in deep, to exhilarating moans. Ooh, it feels damn good, causing me to moan even louder. I tightly grab my ass with my left hand and dig my fingernails into my inner thigh. I give a little stimulation around my anus.

I rapidly stroke my frontal wall and reach my G-spot. I move my hand to spread my lips even wider to get good penetration with my fingers. I clench my buttocks as the dildo moves further and deeper in and out of me. I moan with great pleasure. The feelings are overwhelming. Clawing the bed and closing my eyes, this is bliss. My own natural lubricant is dripping hot as I quiver and shake. I'm loving myself! With my hand, I softly caress my right nipple. I'm working magic with my new expert touches. Erotic pleasures spiral deep within me. This sexual self-stimulation is greater than anything I've ever experienced before. My legs tremble and straighten. I scream in delight as I release my deep orgasm, feeling my hot juices run through me. Oh, it feels so good! It makes me feel so relaxed, like a coiled spring unwinding.

There are no witnesses to my pleasure, only my own smiles and delights. My eyes sparkle as I realize that I can control my own enjoyment and the intensity of it. I feel no guilt.

I think the Greeks got it right when they considered it a safety valve against destructive sexual frustration. It's an untold secret that's never discussed among my mommy friends or family, but I can accept myself and feel complete.

My new motto should be "An orgasm a day keeps the doctors away," because this is damn good stuff. Female masturbation is the key to feeling sexually satisfied when there is no available cock, and I wonder why women don't masturbate as frequently as men to release the tension. As I'm finishing myself off, I think of "I Touch Myself" by The Divinyls. I feel like I'm discovering a map to my sexual freedom. The orgasm could be my new fad diet. Each orgasm that I give myself could take inches off my love handles. The afterglow will do wonders for my face and confidence. Beaming inside and out, I feel a sense of contentment. I have my own higher power close to me. I am a sensual woman with sexual desires. Who would have thought that it would take me until middle age to find and discover this intimate self-pleasure? My inner self is fulfilled and gratified. Grinning like a Cheshire cat, I turn onto my side and fall into a deep sleep.

I awaken a few hours later feeling calm and relaxed. No one can tell me what to do, my father or my ex-boss. I'm going to do what I want and when I want. I pull on my tight blue jeans, a black cotton top and fetch my riding boots. Running towards the door, I grab my car keys and head for my next challenge. I decide to satiate my next impulsive need by trying my luck at the Riverside casino. I know I will be lucky because God is in control of the wheel. I surrender myself to this notion. I've watched hours of Poker Night and the World Series of Poker on television, where one guy won $10 million. I feel like it's going to be my lucky night. I am destined to win. It's unlikely that I will have to write $10,000 checks to cover my gambling addiction like some of the losers that appear from time to time in the papers. I don't even have that in my bank account. Besides, betting on sporting games isn't my thing. For me, the real action is at the card tables. It looks easy enough to play. It can't be too hard to master. I know I can be a pro, just like the current surge of celebrities they show playing, and thanks to my escapades in the Big Easy I have an ill-gotten $500 bankroll.

There is nothing quite like the initial thrill of entering a casino. With its low upper lighting, the room is illuminated by its colorful and brightly lit slot machines at eye level, enticing you in with their flashing lights and hypnotic sounds, offering you the possibility of making your fortune.

The atmosphere has a tendency to suck and draw you into its timeless environment. With just one spin of the wheel, throw of the dice or turn of the card, it has the potential to change your financial life forever.

As I head towards the card tables, I see that almost all the slot machines have someone playing them, mostly seniors, wired into them with their loyalty cards, pressing spin buttons in the hope of being the next one to hit the jackpot. It seems such a solitary pursuit, whereas as I look to my right I see raucous crowds gathered around the Craps table, cheering and groaning at each roll of the dice, a much more social game. Each to their own I suppose.

The 5 C's Challenge

I see a blackjack table with a couple of free places and an attractive young male dealer, whose name is Jimmy according to the black lettering on the gold badge on his lapel, so I take a seat there. I wait for the current hand to finish before indicating that I would like to participate, and pass a $100 bill towards him, in return for forty casino chips.

Almost everyone knows how to play blackjack, but in order to play and win I need a basic strategy, which I will try to stick to, although I know that sometimes I'm likely to feel impulsive and deviate from. Splitting a pair of nines is usually a good idea unless the dealer's face-up card shows a seven or ten. Always hit with soft thirteen, or stand with seventeen or over, irrespective of what the dealer shows. I'd rather stand on hard thirteen versus the dealer's six and hope he busts his hand.

I'm determined that I won't pussyfoot around with my decisions. My sole mission will be to beat the dealer. I like being the one to dominate and stay on top, especially now that I've found my confidence. It's not my thing to bust and go home broke. I'm looking for strong hands to favor me. I know I can go higher than the dealer. I'm up for a match and rising to the occasion. I'm not looking for a push, only a straight win will satisfy my desire.

The cards are dealt face up and I stick firmly to my basic betting strategy. I win a few hands and lose a few. Lots of ups and downs, chips getting passed backwards and forwards across the playing area.

I find it intriguing when a fellow gambler signals a hit by pointing to his cards, or scratching or waving toward himself in an upside down beckoning movement. I guess this is done so that the dealer can be in no doubt as to the player's intention. I find myself doing the same thing, pointing to my cards for a hit, and waving my hands sideways over my cards when I want to stand.

The dealer deals and I'm dealt a natural twenty-one. I love the thrill of winning. While Jimmy is dealing the cards

I notice his cute smile and perfectly manicured fingernails. He must be all of twenty years younger than me. I wonder what it would be like to be fucked hard by someone so young, but his mannerisms suggest that I'm not his type.

Half an hour in and a couple of drinks later I'm up a little, and decide to let my latest win ride. I'm dealt eleven and decide to take a further risk by doubling down, so I place an additional bet at the side of my original bet, and I'm dealt a third card, a jack. No push here, the dealer makes nineteen so I win a big pot and decide that it's time for me to move on. I thank and tip Jimmy and head upstairs to the poker room.

After living with my ex for many years, I've learned the art of a solid bullshit technique. He could lie to my face with a smile and twinkle in his eyes. It's hard to shake such manipulation techniques. He was the king of the fake shit and could play anyone, including fooling a priest. He educated me in many ways while I was with him. Some were positive, but mostly I learned the art of taking advantage of others. He was a master manipulator at the best of times. My time is now and I'm up for some advantage play.

I've never played live poker before, so I'm a little nervous, but excited at the same time.

Looking around the busy room I see lots of different characters wearing all sorts of outfits. Many are wearing caps and shades, trying to hide their eyes and emotions. Others are blocking out the room's visual distractions, covering their heads with hoodies or their ears with headphones. Some of these poor sorry souls will get into battles, even when their backs are against the wall and they are losing. They appear to get gratification from torturing themselves, playing when hurt, trying to chase their losses.

I look around for a table with people without these adornments and take a seat. I decide that I'm in it to win, so I convert all my dollars into casino chips. I'm going to have a fun time and put my hours of watching poker and research into practice.

I start off cautiously, betting conservatively. I'm enjoying being in the midst of the casino with all these other players. I watch the pretty cocktail waitresses working the room, as they ensure a constant supply of refreshing drinks. Lots of thoughts float through my mind. I wonder what each of them does for a living. They react so differently to the clientele I'm used to who would openly chat and gossip about their everyday lives. The people sat around me seem so guarded and do not talk about themselves, perhaps in case it gives their opponents too much information. All conversations relate to poker, poker, and poker. I watch how the players interact with each other, their faces as they look at their cards and their reactions when the flops are dealt.

I try to read their reactions and second guess what hands they might be playing. Each hand brings back more thoughts and memories of what I've seen on television and the patterns seem familiar. I pick out some tells. He looks away when he hits his card on the flop, she straightens her messy bet when she's bluffing. After a short while I think I've got enough information to take some of these players out.

The end of the night is near and I'm way ahead. This is too good to be true. I've beaten the house, some of the other players sat at my table, and I've over $1500 worth of chips in my stack. I'm buzzing! A small crowd has gathered around the table and at this moment in time I feel like a celebrity. I can't quit now because I'm on a roll. OK, one more set of blinds and I'm out of here.

The round before my big blind I'm dealt Pocket Cowboys. I try to hide my excitement at having two strong male hole cards in my hand. I limp in, as I'm under the gun, and don't want to give my hand strength away too quickly. One other player calls before the player in cut-off position makes a three-bet. I hesitate for a moment before calling his raise and the other player folds, leaving just the two of us to play this hand head-to-head.

The dealer burns the top card and turns the community cards, which flop a rainbow four, king and nine. I've hit top set and my heart beats hard and fast. There is already nearly $200 in the pot. I bet $100 and the other player raises $100. I have to be in front so far, so I call his raise. The turn card is a seven, which doesn't improve my hand. I'm unsure of the strength of my opponent's hand, especially given how strongly he's been betting, but I see that the pot is now bigger than the amount of chips he has left in front of him.

"I'm all in!" I exclaim.

I've always wanted to say that! I love the thrill and excitement of being on top and in control. I get an immediate call. No holds barred on this one. The winner will definitely take it all.

I feel my heart beating in my throat, and can hardly contain my excitement when he turns over a pair of nines. Only a nine of spades can ruin my chances of a winning pot. The river card is dealt, another four, giving me a winning hand of a full house, kings over fours.

I'm very happy. My lucky day can't be stopped!

I play out the blinds before gathering up my chips. I tip the dealer, leave the table and head towards the cashier's cage in order to cash out a little over $2500!

I check my phone and find a message from Dad, which I conveniently ignore. I can't be bothered with a lecture right now, even though the devil on my shoulder is already giving me the "Dad speech." It's funny but I don't even have to be in his presence to hear his nagging voice trying to tell me the right thing to do. I will end up getting a migraine if I keep on this wavelength.

Wait, my Facebook shows a friend confirmation and a message in my inbox from Derek Phillips. I jump up and down like a giddy cheerleader in high school at game on homecoming night. My face becomes flushed. This distraction is easily welcomed.

His message reads, "Hallo hübsches mädchen. Ich erinnere mich an sie aus deutschen klassen."

I can make out some of the words but my German is way too rusty. I end up relying on the assistance of internet translation software to make sense of his message and giggle at its interpretation.

I respond immediately, typing impulsively. "It has been a long time. I would love to catch up with you."

I make my way to the car with a pocket full of dollars and a big smile on my face and head for home.

The following morning I have another message from Derek. "I'm living in Germany now. If you ever want to make the journey over, look me up! I'm based in Dortmund."

"Oh, wow, he made it to Germany!" I say to myself and while eating breakfast I ponder the possibilities.

I feel very impulsive after my big win at the casino last night. I look at the pile of money on the island and say "What the hell! Why not?"

I reply to his message letting him know that I'm willing and eager to meet up with him. "How about tomorrow?" I enthusiastically type and then sit staring at my screen waiting for an immediate answer.

A short while later I receive the response I was hoping for.

"Sure! That would be great! The nearest airport is in Düsseldorf. Let me know your flight details and I will meet you at the arrival gates. I look forward to seeing you Sammie!"

This is too good to be true!

Before I change my mind, like an impatient and self-gratifying teenager, I search on several travel websites and book the cheapest flight I can find from Providence to Düsseldorf International. I grab my passport, pack a small cabin bag with essentials, send Derek my flight details and head for the airport in pursuit of my dreams.

My first flight takes me to Atlanta, where after a short stopover, and a quick opportunity to change some dollars for Euros, I board the international flight to Germany. I'm so excited. I've never flown so much in such a short period of time. I feel like I'm becoming a seasoned traveler. I figure that I'll be arriving in the early hours of the morning, in my current time zone, so after eating a chicken dinner, served on cheap plastic trays, I try to relax and get a little sleep. The seats don't recline that much and the leg-space is limited, which makes sleeping difficult, and the red flimsy blanket and child-size pillow doesn't offer much comfort for the long overseas flight.

I awaken as the plane is beginning its descent, and glimpse out of the small aircraft window to overlook a new foreign land, all set to be explored. Arriving at terminal C, I make my way to the first restroom I can find in order to freshen up. I change my panties and don a pair of tight black jeans. I splash some water on my face, apply make-up, and put on some fuchsia lipstick to compliment my blue top. I then make my way through security and passport control to the arrivals gate to meet up with Derek and begin my ultimate German adventure.

I don't need binoculars to search for Derek because he's the first person I see that resembles hotness in a delicious, athletic-toned ripped body. As we walk through the arrivals hall I don't really notice the outstanding architecture or the views of the runways. All I notice are his rugged sculpted arms, which remind me of a young Sylvester Stallone in Rocky when he wears a white tank top. His body moves towards me and he greets me with the most amazing smile I've ever seen. I carry a sense of confidence, secrecy and boldness all wrapped into one. He looks at me with his blue eyes and I immediately feel safe and comfortable, which makes me very warm and cozy inside. He is my white knight, here to rescue me. He leans over, gives me a giant kiss and welcoming hug and I'm melted.

"Sammie, it's wonderful to see you! And how you've changed! I never thought that I would catch up with you in Germany, especially after all these years. What a wonderful surprise!"

"Ohh Derek, I would have never thought either, even a few days ago. But here I am!"

I take it all in and light up in his presence.

"Excellent! I will take you on a German tour," he grins.

"I can't wait! I must warn you though, that on my bucket list, I intend to eat all the foods that I couldn't pronounce in German class," I laugh.

"Well this is going to be fun. We have so much to catch up on."

He takes my arm and carries my bag, like a true gentleman who is here to whisk his princess away. I'm caught up in the moment.

"So, are you in the mood for some authentic German food? I know we are going to need some real native meals if we are going to have enough energy for all that I have planned for you."

Derek takes me in his red BMW for a short drive to a local bistro in a residential area. My face is beaming with smiles and I'm enchanted by his beauty and charm. A waitress approaches our table and he takes charge and orders from the lunchtime menu for us.

When the food and drinks arrives, I'm eager to share the Münchner Weisswurst and currywurst. I'd not realized how hungry I am until these delicious plates of food start arriving at our table. All of this traveling has built up my appetite. I want to remember this photo-worthy moment of my German food adventure, so I take a selfie with Derek, eating the meat of his adopted land. The steamed pork sausage or a version of the Bratwurst, sliced and spiced with curry ketchup is tasty and scrumptious.

My sexual fantasies are triggered while sitting across from him. I'm having sexual thoughts of him. I'm free once again and at the hands of a man who treats me like a lady. I put that big long piece of meat between my lips. While drinking my beer, I imagine his white sausage, his own piece of Weisswurst, in my mouth. The taste of the meat feels good and I like every bit of it. It is long and warm. I think of tasting the tip of it first and then shoving the whole lot of it in my mouth. Then I realize in my greediness that I can't down the whole thing in one swift move. It's so different than the best lollipop that I've ever had. I'm also getting off on the psychological aspect of it.

The more beer I drink, the more my thoughts of Derek and I just lying in a bed together, sharing this intimate moment. I don't just want to sit and gaze at it. My brain is in another world. I dreamily think about licking his cock over and over again. I want to relive that first wonderful experience of the initial moment it entered into my mouth. That's the experience I want to treasure.

The hot juice oozes in my mouth and sizzles with a warm inviting heat. I can't get enough and gaze at him keenly with the look of seduction. In these brief moments, he's already got my juices flowing and my passions aroused. I can feel my breathing getting harder and faster as each bite enters my mouth. I could take this traditional Weisswurst meal, served with sweet mustard and a soft pretzel at any time of day. The waitress brings more Weisswurst to the table in a big bowl together with the cooking liquid used for preparation. The whole meal is the art of seduction and tempts me to do things that are beyond my own limits. I'm on such a mental high and I'm enjoying savoring the experience. From the deep squirt of the Weisswurst in my mouth to the smooth flavors that follow, I'm content. The food warms my insides.

I continue to drink more beer to cool myself down as my body temperature rises. The Weisswurst is eaten without the skin, and I follow it up with some Spätzle and some Zwiebelrostbraten Bratkartoffeln. This gravy is simply to die for. I'm deeply surprised that I'm loving every minute of this adventure. Maybe it's because I feel free in a different country, without any limits, or anyone telling me what to do, where or who I have to be. There are no time constraints and no clocks, just me, Derek, and this new dining experience. I'm enjoying being in his company. I'm redefining my own sense of self and it feels good.

We take a trip down memory lane, talking about the good old days of Texas, high school, German classes and what we remember of some of our classmates from those times. He has me in hysterical laughter with some of his stories and anecdotes about what he and his friends used to get up to. I ask him how he ended up living over here. He explains that after graduating he got a job working with a global company as a marketing manager. His abilities and linguistic skills were noted by his boss, who recommended an overseas opportunity to him. The inducement and relocation package were sufficient to seduce him.

"I always loved skiing and some of the best slopes are in Switzerland. I used to travel to Flims or St. Moritz regularly to indulge my passion. Switzerland is such a beautiful country, such stunning scenery, like on a picture postcard, and so mountainous, unlike the flat terrain of Cologne."

He laughs and I see that his eyes have lit up.

I succumb to the appetizing food that's brought to the table. Each dish provides my mouth and taste buds with new delicious oral sensations. I marvel in the surrendering of my mouth to pleasure and the whole surge of passion that comes through me. Right now, that's getting me off more than any physical sensation. I'm having my very own food orgasm. I'm finding it hard not to moan in delight. This feeling is unreal and I'm savoring every moment. I subconsciously start making umm and ahh noises as the flavors light up my palate. It tastes damn good! I don't want to appear messy and have any of the juices trickle down my chin, but I see no shame in front of Derek because we're having fun and we have a connection.

God I'm relaxed and it feels so good! The food is not just a tangy and rich experience, but it's something symbolic and international in nature. All these feelings are so foreign to me, but are now defining the new me. I've gained confidence that I won't stumble or fall. I feel different, changed, changing. Oh, how I wish that my ex could see me now! In fact, if he could see me, I don't think he would recognize me. I'm not even sure that I would recognize myself. I never felt comfortable or had this sense of freedom with him. He was always so demanding and controlling.

I'm savoring this moment and it's goddamn good. This relaxed and euphoric state of mind gives me pleasure. Maybe I'm a late bloomer who has never had opportunity come knocking at my door to experience life. Who knew such desires and feelings existed? But damn, this is so hot and unexpected. It's not like the usual "lip buzz" or "back of the mouth buzz," it's one great experience of a lifetime. I'm a fighter and fighting to regain my identity. But who is the real me? Does anyone ever really know?

We go back to Derek's car and my own clairvoyant style can't believe it. Is it my own destiny, dumb luck, or fate? I'm not sure which if any of those that I believe in. My faith and course of life has been tested so many times. I know I've been battered in the past and especially by the divorce process. But this isn't the time to think about such things. I'm now given new opportunities and experiences. Is this a spot of redemption? Will I have a second chance and opportunity? Here lies one in terms of Derek's car. Next thing to break out of the box is to drive really fast. In the bright light of day, his red BMW is the answer to my challenge. I've always wanted to drive on the autobahn. I must be dreaming because this can't be a real experience.

Things like this only happen in the movies. I giggle and try to impress him by speaking German.

"Haben sie einen schnellen red BMW, dass ich auf der autobahn fahren?"

He laughs at my attempt. I can tell by his expression that I didn't quite get it right.

"You mean you'd like to go for a drive somewhere?" he responds with a cheeky smile.

I nod in eager anticipation. I feel relaxed and at ease with him. His accepting qualities comfort and embrace me. Even though we are now living on different continents, we share a connection and a past. This is the tie that binds us. I'm genuinely happy and I haven't felt that in a long time. I know that he isn't going to be the great love of my life, but at this moment I am really enjoying his company. Derek continues to enchant me with his eyes and smiles.

"How about we drive down the autobahn?" he says giving me a wink.

I'm loving his comfortable flirtatious style.

Coyly, I smile back, "Yes, but only under certain conditions."

I'm not ready to make things easy for him.

He stares directly at me and engages in my playfulness.

"Miss Sam, I didn't know you require such conditions. I am intrigued."

Laughing with him, I wink back, "I want to be in the driver's seat."

My confidence surprises even me. I know that I don't need an international driver's permit to cover the territory.

"That can easily be arranged. I will get us out of the city and you can be free to manage the way."

I love how accommodating he is. In my past life I used to have to struggle to get a man to agree with me or take me seriously. With my ex everything was a battle. I think he forgot how to have normal conversations with me. Towards the end of our marriage we only existed together but never really communicated with each other, leading desperate lives with different thoughts that never agreed.

Derek takes me around the city and drives along streets with names that I can't even pronounce. I love being the passenger, sitting back and enjoying the passing scenery. At the same time I have a strong desire to get behind the wheel, rev the engine and move at my own pace.

Derek pulls over at a rest stop. This man is really genuine and will actually grant my wish. It must be my lucky day. Can he be the one that listens to me and takes me seriously? I quickly switch seats with him before he changes his mind and realizes that this may not be a good idea. Sitting in the black leather driver's seat is such a thrill. Derek touches my hand and gives me a quick tutorial of where the gears and controls are. I'm a quick learner and I feel comfortable in my new position.

I see signs for autobahn 57 and I'm eager and excited. Derek is pleased and encouraging. The control of the engine and the fast speed is a turn on. I love being the one in control at the wheel. Being new to this experience, I start off cautiously as the engine feels so powerful. The BMW hugs the road and is a smooth ride.

Derek stares at me the whole time. I can make out his facial expressions despite his sunglasses.

"Why Sammie, I know you want to go faster. Show me what you've got. You know this engine has a lot more power than you're using."

His voice is hypnotic. His inviting charm encourages me to take a little risk. I put the pedal to the metal and the scenery begins to fly past us. I shudder to think about how many cars we've passed. I'm far removed from my homeland and beyond my normal limits. Crazy, stupid speed is what it's all about. I clench my hands firmly to the wheel and take control. I'm a force to be reckoned with.

"Wow, you are cooking now," he chuckles at me.

"I think I can go a little faster," I say, while pushing my limits and firmly pressing the gas.

"Now you're talking. That's what I like to see. A girl who really knows what she wants and takes control."

I can see that testing my boundaries is exciting him. We race down the road and a feeling of freedom runs down my spine. I'm feeling in my groove, listening to the growl of the engine, as I accelerate and overtake other cars.

Derek puts his hand on mine and says, "You are a bad, bad girl, but I like it! I think we will have to go on more adventures together."

"That sounds good, real good, and I could get used to this lifestyle."

I'm pleased with how things are looking and there is no turning back now. I've officially left my comfort zone and am now living life "out of the box." What a daring maneuver under the prompting of Derek.

~ Recipe 6 ~
Expanding Boundaries

Prep time:	Two days
Serve:	Many

This recipe is for those that enjoy a good time and the indulgences in life. This recipe is not for the rigid. Some may want more from this recipe and yet still not be fully satisfied. Some will find it hard to stop. Set your desires free to fully experience this recipe.

Creativity:	Experiment with a woman
Cost:	Take psychedelic drugs
Culinary:	Eat chocolate
Culture:	Pole dance
Connect:	Reach out to Dad

For a special treat, Derek takes me to the Imhoff-Stollwerck Chocolate museum in Cologne. He's on a mission to please me with a good time. I never knew such a place existed. The museum sits right on the edge of the River Rhine, and has been designed in the shape of a ship. It's certainly an impressive construction of steel and glass. As soon as we enter the building we are met with the sweetest chocolate aroma, such a pleasurable fragrance!

I make it my mission to enjoy and indulge in my "Chocolate Day."

In all my years of eating chocolate, I had no idea what a cocoa tree looked like, much less seen pods growing from the trunk, until seeing some in the museum's tropicarium. As we walk through the museum, we follow the story of how the beans within the pods are dried and processed, all the way through to reaching the factory production line and being turned into the product we are so familiar with. I find the history and processing from bean to bar fascinating. It's funny how having a better understanding changes my perception. I will never look at chocolate in the same way again.

I can't wait to sample some freshly made melted chocolate from the large golden chocolate fountain! When I do so, it's the best I've ever tasted. Absolutely delicious and yummy! After testing this exquisite melt-in-the-mouth taste sensation, I suggest that we head to the gift shop in order to purchase some chocolate for my journey. Wow, there is so much to choose from! So many different shapes, sizes and flavors. I'm like a kid in a candy store, literally!

"Would you like a drink?" Derek asks. "There is a café over there."

"Sure!" I say, new chocolate purchases in hand, and we head in that direction.

He orders two fresh warm chocolate croissants and hot chocolate drinks, and we take them and sit out on the terrace, overlooking the Rhine. From our vantage point we have great views of the bridges spanning the wide river and the small boats sailing by. He seems to take delight in seeing me so interested and happy.

He turns to me and softly says, "Tell me, is that the best way to wet your taste buds, Sammie?"

I giggle, "You are beginning to know me so well and how to please me."

I'm feeling relaxed and really enjoying his company. He smirks, "We Americans are all alike. Fast cars and chocolates are easy ingredients to satisfy us."

I blush at his suggestion. Am I that predictable? We finish our drinks, and leave the museum.

Where to next, I wonder?

As we are heading back to his car, his phone rings and I can see he's answering a text message. His face suddenly changes. He gives me another one of his smiles, but this one looks a little forced.

"You know Sammie, this has been a great journey so far, but I don't want to mislead you."

"What are you talking about?" I ask as I turn to face him.

"Well this has been fun and all, and certainly not what I expected."

He looks serious now.

"What you getting at?"

I think I already know the answer as I try to interpret the telling expression on his face.

He looks down and isn't making eye contact with me anymore.

"It has nothing to do with you. It's just something that I have to take care of. You know, responsibilities and stuff. Things were already in motion before you came along."

I look at him and realize that I've gotten my hopes up again, and am once more living in a fairytale world. I wanted to escape from everything, but in my desire to escape, I had forgotten what was real. Of course he has responsibilities and "stuff," a.k.a. another woman. She probably has long straight blonde hair, beautiful big blue eyes and giggles at his every word to capture his attention. She will have been in his life long before I came along. His allegiance is with her. I was a fool to think that Derek's charm would be just for me. When will I ever learn? What a set up for disappointment! His blonde bombshell will be waiting for him in a boudoir, wearing some fancy sexy negligee. I'm sure they'll enjoy taking selfies together, or that he'll have his camera willingly aimed at her beauty.

"Can I drop you off somewhere?"

I now know his plans are to dash and run. To bail out on me before I even get started.

"No it's OK. I'm a big girl. I can take care of myself." I grab my bags from his car and turn the other way so he can't see my disappointment. My face is flushed and I feel foolish. I'm a strong and stubborn woman who never seems to learn from my countless mistakes. I've no time for being the other woman, and the image of Derek with someone else can't escape my head.

"I'm so very sorry. I don't know what else to say, but I really have to go."

I cut it short. I don't want to have anything else to do with this conversation. I've had enough of it, and enough of him. Why do I get myself mixed up in a fantasy world that can't come true? In my own marriage, I was starved emotionally and sexually and craved a companion that could offer me fulfillment. It was lacking in so many ways and now I'm lost trying to understand and explain it.

Desire for attention clouded my judgment. I knew Derek would not fill that void or gap. He quite clearly has deep commitments elsewhere. I'm sure I would always be his last priority in life and never fit in. He will never know the amount of desire that I have for him. A wasted encounter that has left me dumbfounded. For a brief moment it was fun and adventurous, unlike anything I had ever experienced before. I don't know who I was trying to kid.

Instead of crying, I turn to my solace, chocolate and church. I want what I want and I want it now. I grab a heavenly dark chocolate with hazelnut candy bar for my immediate fix, as I hear the BMW's engine growl quietly into the distance.

All alone in a foreign country, what shall I do now? I amble along the side of the Rhine, taking in the panoramic views, while trying to find some direction.

To my left I see the grand Romanesque architecture of St Martin church with its stunningly impressive crossing tower. I'm drawn by its majesty, so turn and head towards it. I wander down a narrow street into a large cobbled market square, where I pass a fountain and pretty pastel-colored buildings, before seeking the main entrance to the building. I can always turn to the church in my hour of need. It's a place that offers me shelter when I'm lost. For a moment, I can find peace and sanctuary here.

I enter the church through large wooden outer doors, surrounded overhead by impressively ornate arch stonework. I stop and read a large multi-lingual sign attached to the wall, telling a brief fascinating history of its existence. I wander down the aisles, looking at paintings and religious statues that decorate its interior, before coming across stunningly beautiful and colorful floor mosaics depicting the eight Beatitudes, surrounding a raised altar in the crossing transept.

I walk to the nave and take a seat, gazing in awe at the high ceilings and the stained glass windows which light the space perfectly as the sun shines through the colored panes. I try to pray, but can't. Religious guilt always seems close at hand. My faith offers convenience, but right now I cannot find the conviction that I belong. I sit for a few moments, feeling uneasy and unsure at my current predicament. I don't know where to turn. It's easier for me to run than to face the truth.

I walk aimlessly around the old town looking for a sign for what to do next. Looking at my reflection in a glass window, I wonder what lecture my dad would give me if he saw me now. I need to hear his voice to guide me. I'm tired and unhappy but I know that he will understand. The song "Landslide" by Fleetwood Mac runs through my head. My dad can be my mirror when things get rough. He will be brutally honest when I need it and push me to my limits. We are mutually stubborn and understand where our support systems need to be for each other. He has a voice that can be harsh but whose words ring true.

I find an internet café to Skype him. The phone rings and I have a funny feeling and almost chicken out. He picks up quickly.

"Yeah, Hello?" he answers.

"Hi Daddy, it's me."

"Where in God's name are you? I've been trying to get hold of you. Your mother is worried sick about you, and Jess and Josh say they haven't heard from you. What are you playing at?" he scolds me.

Man, I didn't think it would be this bad. My reality starts to dawn on me. I take deep breaths, swallowing each one and sit there cold faced. I'm about to shut off from this lecture. How I dreamed that he would just comfort me with open arms. I can't deal with this confrontation.

"Dad, I'm OK. Really I am. I'm just away for a few days visiting friends."

I don't think I can even convince myself with that tone.

"The kids will be alright. I just need some more time."

"Time? What do you mean, time? Where the hell are you?"

His voice is getting angry and frustrated. He's scolding me again. I'm his little girl who has done wrong.

"Dad. Please, I don't need this."

Tears begin rolling down my cheeks. He won't understand. I thought I could make an honest attempt at reaching out, but instead I'm confronted with negativity. I'm not ready to deal with this.

"I will tell you what you need, and it's all right here. You can't just walk away from it you know. I went to the salon and found out you'd quit. What are you playing at? Why do I have to hear this from someone else?"

His voice is bitter and his words sting.

This is too much for me. I'm on overload. People are starting to stare at me. I feel very self-conscious. I just want to run away from this conversation and this situation. This isn't for me. In my second attempt, I shut down on him again.

"Dad, tell the kids I love them and I will be in touch soon."

I hang up, bringing the conversation to an abrupt end. A man with bad boy facial features and dreadlocks, wearing an unconventional outfit which looks like it's come straight from a Paris runway, is staring at me from the other side of the room. All I can do is cry. My tears are flowing like a long river of sadness. Tears are the universal language of hurt and pain, numb feelings are the barrier protecting my weak heart. I want to bury myself, but there is nowhere for me to hide. The man approaches me, and in a thick German accent introduces himself.

"My name is Nickolaus. Looks like you have seen better days."

My eyes turn to meet his. I look at him, like I'm a wounded lamb. His bright green eyes comfort me and I'm taken aback by his direct nature. I know my dad wouldn't approve of this man, with his badass look and an unshaven lion's mane of a beard, but beneath it I see a warm caring smile, and genuine compassion.

"Let me help you get your mind off it," he says confidently, while handing me a tissue.

Half smiling, I thank him for his kind gesture.

"My name is Sam."

"That's cool. I see that you are wearing blue. How fitting Sam! So I can at least take you for a drink, right? This is a very interesting café but I think we perhaps need to go elsewhere."

I'm taken in by his charm. His insight captivates me, and I'm curious. I don't have a curfew, so I pick up my belongings and follow.

We walk a couple of blocks to his first floor apartment in the city. He puts some music on, passes me a bottle of beer, and we sit next to each other on his brown worn out leather couch.

"So tell me about yourself Sam. How long are you staying in Germany?"

I confess to him that I flew over on a whim in order to catch up with an old school friend, but that it didn't work out as I'd hoped. I also tell him a little about my beautiful children and my acrimonious divorce.

He sits patiently listening to me talk.

"You want a smoke?" he asks.

I don't even think, wanting to join in whatever he does, because I know he has a comforting ear.

"Sure, I don't mind," I reply.

He puts his hand into his pocket and pulls out what looks like a hand-rolled spliff. My eyes open wide in surprise.

"Is that what I think it is?"

He nods and gives a telling smile. Aww shit, he means the real deal! In all my years, I've never touched the stuff. I've never had the urge to smoke it myself, and never really understood its appeal.

It's not like I'm from the baby boomer generation who smoked in their teens, or on a multiple-decade layoff and need to get my feet wet again. It isn't even legal in my state, even though it regularly tops the list of illicit drug usage. I've been to parties where one or two of my friends have tried it, and I remember smelling the sweet scent of cannabis wafting through the air when I went to see the Grateful Dead in concert years ago, but by and large, drug use has never been a part of my life or my social circle. But at this moment I'm not in mommy mode anymore, and I'm receptive to new experiences and experimentation.

I've always felt guilty about trying "bad" things, but hell, if it doesn't harm anyone in the process, then where's the problem? There are a numerous United States presidents who have admitted using marijuana at some point in their lives, and the consequences to them weren't severe. If the Commander-in-chief can have a toke, why can't I do so without worry or guilt?

He flicks open a Zippo lighter, with an image of a cannabis leaf silhouetted by the colors of the Jamaican flag, and lights up his spliff. He inhales deeply, causing its tip to glow vibrant orange, before exhaling slowly, blowing out vast amounts of smoke through pursed lips. I can see that he's an experienced toker, and I'm his little rookie.

"Here, this will take the edge off those worries of yours," he says, passing it to me.

I'm nervous and anxious all rolled into one. I hold it between thumb and forefinger and put it to my quivering pink lips.

I take a really small drag and don't hold it for long. It has a sweet herbal taste. I immediately feel a warm pleasant tingle in my throat and lungs.

I see that Nickolaus doesn't rush me, or make me toke until I choke.

I inhale some more. The competitor in me wants to chief it. I'm not sure about regulating my hits as it seems foreign to me, but the more I inhale the better it seems to make me feel. I'm no regular Bob Marley but I feel crazy ass sensations as I take one massive puff.

A moment later the intensity hits me. Its potency is out of this world, and I'm quickly getting baked out of my mind. I feel somewhat slightly light-headed, and have this strange sensation that my whole body is being lifted up off the couch. I gasp for breath, breathing in deeply, as my mind experiences the sensation of getting high.

My heart starts beating faster but I'm not sure if it's because I'm nervous, or due to the sensations that are rushing through my body. Suddenly I panic, that I might be having a fucking heart attack.

I'm in outer space and not moving around anything. Random objects are flashing bright colors. I think there is a secret cop videotaping me and hiding right here. That person is going to show the fucking world that I'm smoking my first joint. I fear that I may collapse, stop breathing, and blackout. Oh my God, oh my God! I breath in and out, deep breaths, deep breaths.

I look around to see that I'm still on the couch, not mystically floating above it, and see Nickolaus chilling beside me, feeling good. I rejoin the real world, and take a swig of beer then another toke and begin to regain a sense of inner calm. My inwardly vertical journey seems to have reached a plateau, which feels incredible. I feel a smile growing on my face, and a state of elation. Wow, so this is what it's like to feel high!

"Stayin' Alive" by the Bee Gees is playing on the sound system. My stumbling feet move off the couch, headed for the kitchen, in search of tasty treats. Anything with chocolate will do for my craving. I'm on a search and destroy mission for chocolate. After nine seconds of smoking some weed, food is now my friend, because that's all I'm thinking about. I will eat everything and anything in my sight. I've a strong desire for chocolate chip cookies and pretzels. Any random combination will do, or whatever is in the fridge.

I can't stop laughing, and I've a serious case of the munchies. I want to know how his toaster works, and does it work the same way as an American toaster? I've a fucking brilliant idea but the words don't come out of my mouth, only more laughter.

Whoa! I'm back in Nickolaus' apartment and I'm still hungry for chocolate. Fuck! I need to eat right now. I feel like hours have gone by. I'm not even sure of the time anymore, or how long I've been stood looking at the toaster. I return to the couch after my kitchen raid, with packets of chips, cookies and chocolate bars, which I place on the coffee table in front of me. I then look in bemusement at the carrier bag with

"Schokoladenmuseum" emblazoned on it at the side of where I've been sitting.

I burst out laughing, telling Nickolaus that I've just spent ages turning his kitchen upside-down in search of chocolate, while completely forgetting the goodies that I bought several hours earlier. How we laugh!

My mouth feels dry as I'm in my stoner bubble. I start coughing, but I'm not sure if it's a normal reaction or just my nervousness.

Nickolaus smiles and says, "You gotta cough to get off!"

I feel so good. He passes me another joint and I take another hit, or three. Hell yeah! My mind is definitely ripped. I see our reflection in his mirror and wonder why his eyes aren't as red as mine. Another telltale sign I'm a newbie. He now knows for sure that I'm an amateur smoker by my foolish reactions. I notice that I'm speaking slower but I'm not sure whether it's because I'm intently concentrating on every last word that he's saying to me. My ears are ringing a little and my body temperature rises.

Everything is slowing down and I find the deep tone of his voice very sexy. I feel lazy, happy and in a dreamlike state. An altered state of reality. I look at the carpet in the room. Its textured pattern and autumnal colors appear vibrant, and capture my attention. When I close my eyes I can actually see the music. I see rainbow colored dragons and intensely realistic imagery, like being conscious in a dream, and I finally "get" the music. I never really thought about music like this before, or the heightened awareness that a little weed can elicit within the brain, and it's fucking fantastic. It's a strange mix of mild euphoria with the desire to eat treats. A wave of butterflies hits me from out of nowhere. My body feels heavier for some reason, like something's drained the strength out of me.

While we sit on his couch, indulging in pot, beer and munchies, he puts a Cheech and Chong movie on. It's fucking hilarious. I find myself giggling uncontrollably at the movies dialog. I'm fucking high as shit and laughing at everything I see. I begin to see why people want to experience this sensation, and understand why some can become addicted to it. This is extraordinary!

A feeling of euphoria and goodwill rushes over me. My goodwill ambassador is this German guy named Nickolaus who I know very little about, but he's my friend. A calmness comes over me. My stresses are all but gone now. This is one damn good high!

"Sam, I want to show you what life is all about."

He moves closer to me.

"I thought I knew a lot about life before I met you, but I, umm, never experimented with it, or went beyond my limits, or comfort zone and stuff," I reply.

My eyes can't seem to stay focused.

"If you are willing to trust me, I will help you discover your inner freedoms."

"Nickolaus, with you I feel free."

I feel so content and ready to expose all to him.

"Good, Sam. Here is to the good life, and finding and releasing your inner desires."

I smile at him, close my eyes and fall into a blissfully relaxing sleep on the couch. I wake up to find that Nickolaus had put a blanket over me while I slept. I get up and decide to take a nice refreshing shower. I head to the bathroom and run the shower until the water is hot enough, and then jump right in.

As I begin wetting my hair, Nickolaus comes into the bathroom, and enters the shower cubicle, standing right behind me. I'm startled and surprised, but feel really relaxed in his company, so I don't say a word. He grabs some liquid soap, squirts it onto a natural sea sponge and starts to lather my back, rubbing firmly up and down. Mmm, that feels great! Then, taking some shampoo, he gently massages it into my hair and scalp.

He then starts rubbing my shoulders in a circular motion, slowly making his way inwards and towards my neck. This slow sensuous massage feels so good as the warm water runs down my body.

He takes the showerhead in his hand, tilts my head back, ever so slightly, and begins rinsing off the shampoo. I close my eyes to avoid getting soapy water in them, and find that the physical sensations are intensified by the temporary removal of my visual sense. He then takes some conditioner and lathers it into my scalp.

I've never been pampered like this in the shower before. He grabs the soap, and with lathered hands guides and glides them around the contours of my shoulders and arms, and then massages my shoulders some more, then reaching for the showerhead, he rinses off the conditioner.

Grabbing the sea sponge he squirts more liquid soap onto it and then crouches down to clean my calves, thighs, inner thighs, "ooh, yeah!"

As he moves his firm hands up my legs it sends chills down my spine. I could melt as my legs turn to jelly. He stands upright and turns me around to face him. I stare intensely at him looking for a signal for how I should respond. I'm not sure if he really wants me, wants to play with my body, or could it possibly be that he just wants to spoil me? The sexual tease excites me, as I allow him to explore my body. He gives me no clues, but keeps his hands busy. He lathers more soap, massaging my breasts, and running his soapy thumbs over my nipples. He moves them in a circular motion and I'm aroused with pleasure. I smile and close my eyes again, just waiting for his next move. His hands trace the contours of my curvy body. Every inch of me is feeling the gentle touch of his caress.

His movements are slow and deliberate, as he looks at and analyzes the shape of my body, studying it in great detail. I hold my hands in the air, like I'm surrendering myself to him. His fingers intertwine with mine for a moment, holding them tight. He then begins kissing them, sucking each one deeply into his mouth. He's dominant and I'm at his mercy. He changes the setting of the showerhead to pulsate mode and moves it to my inviting pussy. He waves the head back and forth directly hitting his target. The pleasurable sensation of spurting warm liquid hitting my pussy gets my insides all hot and wet.

He replaces the showerhead, takes the sponge and with more soap rubs my pussy, stroking it with his masculine hands. His pinky finger gently rubs against my clitoris, and he reaches for my nipple with his other hand. He plays with my nipples, gently twisting them counter and clockwise. It feels so good!

He surprises me with a slap to my ass for good measure and I immediately re-open my eyes, smile and nod my head in silent approval.

It's as if he's checking to make sure I'm paying attention to all the details of his pleasures. He knows I'm feeling amazing but he doesn't force himself on me. My impulses say that I want him, but he won't allow me to touch him in that manner. I'm submissive to the pleasures that he's showering me. His hands tease my body making me want him to never stop.

He turns the water off and grabs a plush white Egyptian cotton towel to wrap around me. He pats my body down and puts some lotion into the palm of his hand, so as to softly moisturize my back. I'm feeling like a princess with the amount of pampering and pleasing I'm receiving. He kisses my cheek, takes my hand and walks me to his bedroom. I'm unsure why he hasn't tried to fuck me, and am still curious as to his motives. He doesn't say a word but curls his finger at me and pats the bed. I lay face down and he rubs lotion onto my relaxed body. I'm so comfortable that I close my eyes and almost immediately fall back to sleep.

Nickolaus wakes me up with a platter of delicious Bauernfruhstuck, and a glass of chilled orange juice. Breakfast in bed! I look out of the bedroom window to see the sun rising, and figure it's the start of a new day. My appetite gets the better of me, so I eat until my tummy feels satisfied. Life doesn't get any better than this. I feel as though my soul has been rescued and this is exactly what I needed. This distraction is a welcome break from my own reality. Nickolaus smiles at me like a teacher, proud of his student who has just received an A+. After I've eaten my fill, he brings over a mirror and hands it to me.

"Sam, I want you to see what I see," he says in his sexy tone.

"What are you talking about?"

"Sam, you are beautiful. But I don't think you have given yourself the time to appreciate your own self. I want you to look at your entire body, the way I appreciated you in the shower earlier."

Laughing and embarrassed, I roll my eyes.

"Are you fucking kidding me?"

"Just follow my direction," he says, while looking intently at me. "Look in the mirror Sam. Look at your body in detail."

I get up out of bed and awkwardly oblige his request. I look at my reflection and can't believe it's me. It's my natural face in the glass. There is no make-up or barrier in my way. My face has changed and I swear I look like I've lost a few years. Usually I would feel dissatisfaction with the growing wrinkles or bags under my eyes. These flaws seem less apparent right now. The pureness of my face is remarkable, despite it facing the elements all these years. I look again at my reflection and smile at myself. The fairytale of Snow White has long been ingrained in my mind. This is no magic mirror but it is my own reflection. For the first time in a long time, I can say that I like what I see, and what I see is me. My lips are pink and soft. My skin appears creamy and vibrant. My hair is bright and the blonde golden. My blue eyes are radiant and sparkle like sapphires. I'm beaming with the grace of my own beauty. Almost like meeting a stranger for the first time, I gaze at the introduction of this beautiful woman reflected back at me.

"Your freckles make you unique and add character to your appearance. See your neck? Hold it high, for it's the stand which holds your beautiful face."

I tilt the mirror and lift my head up, like a giraffe reaching for the tastiest leaves. I examine my neck and see hundreds of tiny light brown freckles that I've never really studied before. I smile, feeling flattered by his words and his attention to detail.

"Now look at your shoulders. They are the strong beams for you to hold your head up high and be proud of who you are and what you have been through."

I move the mirror to my shoulders and square them. He moves closer to me.

"Look at that beautiful curved bone, which is your clavicle."

I see the raised ridge on my upper chest and feel myself standing taller.

"Have you ever been sweetly kissed in that sexy valley of yours?"

He moves his middle finger gently along the lines of my right shoulder sending goose bumps down my spine.

"Next, we have your lovely breasts which would have even inspired Auguste Rodin. He would have sculpted every inch of you in plaster, and had you forged in bronze."

Looking down at my breasts, I touch and cup each one gently with the palm of my hand. They are quite weighty. I lift my left breast and notice a few freckles and raised brown moles underneath, which I've never noticed before. I wonder how long I've had these? I run my fingers over them and consider whether I should get them checked out. What if I've skin cancer? My ex never mentioned them to me before. Did he ever discover my body and pay attention to every detail like I'm doing now? I examine my Saint tattoo and reflect on the lesson I learned from that experience.

Although the Fleur-de-lis is associated with royalty, French monarchy, team logos, military badges and exciting places like New Orleans, for me it's now a permanent reminder of the foolish mistake I made, being one of Pete's conquests. What a silly fool I was to follow his lead! Nickolaus quickly distracts me getting me to focus on my body.

"Move down to your belly, which should be celebrated, as it not only holds the nourishment to energize you, but your lovely children grew in that area as well."

I reflect upon my pregnancies and how I glowed when I carried my children. I was forever rubbing my belly and looking at how my body changed in shape and size throughout. I don't think that I've rubbed my belly since those days.

"You know I was obsessed with my baby-belly and showed it off to the world. I must have taken a picture of my profile every month of my pregnancy."

"I bet you haven't taken pictures recently of your belly, have you?" he questions with a seductive smile.

My laugh stutters at the thought.

"That would be crazy!"

"What is so crazy about that? You should cherish your body. It's your temple and you should worship it."

He gives me a tight bear hug which both comforts me and reminds me how much I've let myself go in the last few years. I feel like I haven't paid enough attention to myself.

"Now let's look at that lovely pussy and sexy ass of yours. Have you ever gotten up close and personal with your pussy?"

He smiles, gently patting my pussy and rubbing my ass.

I laugh nervously. "Umm, no."

He puts his hand between my inner thighs and gestures that I spread my legs a little, and then takes the mirror and moves it downwards, angling it so that I can clearly see the reflection of my shiny red clitoris.

"Mmm, look how beautiful that is. Take time to study your sexual anatomy, and identify your parts. Get to know yourself."

I've always passed my reflection in the mirror, but I don't think I've actually studied my own pussy. I look at the folds of fat and skin and think to myself that I should give myself a bikini wax to make my bits look smooth.

If you had pictures of pussies in a line up I don't think I would be able to recognize my own. Each pussy is as unique as each woman's face, all being of different shapes, colors and sizes. My vagina was always surrounded with mystery. I have deeply-seated inhibitions that were given to me by my family and church. I don't think Mom ever gave me the "sex talk" or discussed my female anatomy. It was never a subject of open discussion. Even among my friends it was something that was snickered about rather than explored and embraced. It's a sad state of affairs that I don't even know my own body up close and personal. My childhood was full of negative messages that did not include being comfortable and proud of playing with myself. Recently, I've given myself multiple orgasms and enjoyed them. I haven't yet explored the contours of my clitoris or the shape of my anus. Where does it begin and end?

I notice the light pink color of my labia minora. I move the mirror towards my labia majora with its pink inner and white outer skin color. Noting the irregular shape of the vaginal orifice and studying it for the first time, I'm amazed at the complexity of my own body. It is not smooth like I imagined. There are lots of bumps and ridges. It is elastic enough to hold a big firm cock. I feel my ramps and smooth edges. My pink pussy reddens in color as I discover it with my fingers, moving them gently and deftly around, guiding my exploration. My vagina looks so delicate but I know from experience, and childbirth, that it's strong and flexible. I examine under the small hood, bending and moving it around, to find the tip and the clitoris. I massage under the hood and it feels like a small cord. Very slowly I find the two "legs," which extend in kind of a wishbone shape behind the outer labia. I'm beginning to find how comfortable I am with my own sexuality. Just touching my clitoris sends pleasurable sensations quivering through my body. I never want that to end now that I've found it. It isn't just a small nub of sensitive skin, it's much more than that. My clitoris is the key to my sexual ejaculation and that's what I'm learning to master. Its sole purpose and function is in providing me with pleasure. Each time I touch myself I'm holding the key to my own desires. I move the mirror to get a good look at the front of the vaginal wall. Finding the inner labia, I feel as though I'm labeling each part of my body. I'm becoming a master of myself. My pussy is unique and damn sexy. I should treat it with dignity and as a thing of beauty.

Nickolaus is beaming with pride as he notices my pleasure. He gets down on his knees and looks up at me with his green eyes. I let him study me and show him my findings. Swaying my hips in a circular motion until they reach the target, I can see his appreciative joy. He massages my buttocks and gently kisses my juicy red pussy, which I hover above his face.

Our eyes connect and we are at one with our thoughts. Lifting my right leg and pointing my toe up in the air to his shoulder, I move like I'm singing "All that Jazz," from the musical Chicago.

"Mister Nickolaus, Let me show you my sexy legs!" I exclaim while doing a theatrical dance pose.

Nickolaus smiles in approval.

"And, don't forget these sexy size nine feet."

"How did you know that?"

He doesn't look like the type who automatically knows your shoe size when you walk up to get your bowling ball at the alley.

"My little secret. I checked out your shoe size Cinderella, in case I found your glass slipper."

He kisses my feet.

I do feel like a princess, from head to toe. I'm shining like a radiant beam of sunshine. But doubt and insecurity begins to rear its ugly head and sneak back into my confidence levels. Nickolaus reads my face and has me figured out.

"Why do you crinkle your forehead when that wave of worry enters your mind? Haven't you learned anything about yourself yet?"

"Thank you Nickolaus, for being so kind. I'm just not used to all this attention." I reply, amazed by his perception.

"Well you need to pay more attention to yourself and your own body, because it's an undiscovered thing of beauty that needs to be admired and loved."

He smiles and gives me a soothing hug.

"Never forget that you are beautiful."

"How did you become so smart and carefree?" I ask curiously, trying to understand his mind.

I'm feeding off of his positive energy and enthusiasm.

"I try to stay open to new adventures and not have predetermined expectations. I don't like to ride the judgmental bandwagon. I free myself to experiences and let go."

"That sounds cool in theory, but…"

My self-limiting thoughts make me hesitate. It's an automatic response, but I've no idea how or when it suddenly became a normal part of my thought process.

"Stop right there! Look back into the mirror, and say this to yourself. I will try something new today, even if I'm afraid of what I might feel."

Glancing at my own wide-open eyes, I nod to myself. I'm ready. It's an overwhelming feeling, that I've granted myself permission to feel good about myself and take pleasure, without guilt.

"Good. Now that we have that understood, let's give the theory a test. How about we get a train to Amsterdam? For around forty euros, we can be there in a little over three hours," he says, looking at his watch. "Are you in?"

My mind doesn't have time to think. Besides Paris, the thought of going to one of the most romantic and beautiful cities in Europe really excites me.

"If you are concerned about the cost, I'm sure we can work something out. I've some connections," he says.

I love his demeanor and confidence. I could learn something from being around such a man.

Wearing simple clothing of a red cotton top, a black lacy circle skirt and warm jacket, I follow his pace. My subconscious desires are kicking in. I gaze up at Nickolaus and find myself walking with him to the station. With only a few essentials packed for our mini journey, we take the Inter-City Express train, which runs regularly and to the timetable, and head from Cologne to Amsterdam Centraal. As we travel towards our destination and across imaginary country boundaries, I look out of the train window at the passing towns and scenery. It's funny how, no matter where you are in the world, things have a comforting familiarity about them. On arrival we head towards a fast food outlet and each get a big meaty burger and fries, compliments of Nickolaus.

He laughs, "I thought you would like some comforts and reminders of home."

I eat the food like there is no tomorrow and look at him sideways in my carefree manner. Nickolaus grabs a handful of fries from my wrapper.

He stares at me for a long time and coyly says "You are my gypsy woman. You're a lovely woman on the move, with no permanent address. You remind me of the Frans Hals painting of the Gypsy Girl, which I remember seeing at the Louvre in Paris. You look sort of bohemian with your cleavage showing and a slightly mischievous smile. At times you have a hardened street smart appearance."

My jaw drops and I immediately stop eating. He notices my dejected stare.

He shakes his head at me, "No, no, you mustn't take it that way. I see that you are sensitive. There is nothing wrong with discovering yourself. You are like a caterpillar turning into a lovely butterfly and finding your wings to fly."

He looks at me with delicate eyes, "You are like a painter yourself, challenging life with your brush, but for you, your brush is the voice inside you. Sam, you have such a soft natural inner beauty."

I start crying and tears begin to run down my face. The thought of being a gypsy doesn't seem glamorous and maybe this is reality staring me in the face. At this moment, I remember that I do not have a job and I'm wandering around with no purpose or direction. I've never thought about, or likened myself to, being a gypsy before. The Stevie Nicks song runs through my head. I'm facing my freedom with a little fear. Learning to live alone again. All I can think of is to keep on traveling. To where, I don't know.

Nickolaus reaches out for my hand.

"Come with me, Sam. Let me show you more about yourself that you never knew existed within."

I reach out my hand, and follow his lead. We exit Amsterdam Centraal and I'm immediately taken in by the impressive architecture.

Nickolaus has my curiosity running wild, as we take a ten minute stroll to Rossebuurt. We walk from the station, across the tramlines, and head up Damrak. On our right we pass the Sexmuseum, on our left, we pass boat docks, filling with tourists eager to experience the canal cruises. As we turn left, we see The Grasshopper in front of us, a large visually impressive building. The sound of music, laughter, and many different languages fill the air.

We walk down narrow cobbled streets, which lead us towards the heart of the Red Light District. Slowly walking up and down the canal and streets in this area leaves nothing to the imagination, as sex blatantly oozes out of every crevice. Stunningly attractive scantily-clad girls pose inside red neon-lit window parlors, most wearing only bikinis to cover their modesty. Some sit serenely on stools waiting for their next client to express an interest, others actively encouraging trade with suggestive body movements, and finger beckoning. All are legally plying their trade.

Different areas offer different women. Some side streets have only black women or larger ladies.

I would have thought that the only people frequenting this area would be dirty old men, out looking for a good time, with a cheap whore. How wrong I am with my assumptions! The tourists in the area are as diverse in appearance as the women in the windows. There are groups of men and women, young and old, and there are couples walking hand in hand. Which group do I fit into? Clearly I'm the one that's most curious to discover more in this liberal and tolerant city. Some are quite clearly titillated by the experience of the legality and openness of the trade, others probably quite surprised that such beautiful women are participating in the world's oldest profession. The working girls certainly do not look anything like the junkie and crack-whores that work the streets in Rhode Island. Every whim and fantasy seem to be catered for. When a deal is made, the punter enters the room through the window door, and the curtain is drawn closed for privacy.

Nickolaus tells me that the windows have neon color-coded lights; red indicates women, purple indicates a man/woman, sometimes with a special surprise between their legs or maybe even an extra piece of meat. I'm like an innocent schoolgirl being put to the front of the line to be taught an eye-popping lesson.

I'm so distracted taking in the sights that I haven't noticed Nickolaus.

He weaves his arm into mine and asks, "How does some dancing sound to you?"

The thought of letting my hair down seems like a no-brainer.

"I'm up for it. Where do you have in mind?"

I feel like I'm being taken on a guided tour.

"How about Rembrandtplein Square? I'm sure it will be something new for you."

I want adventure and a new challenge.

"That sounds fun. I'm in."

I've done some dancing before, but I've a feeling that with Nickolaus it will be something a little different. In no time at all, we are walking alongside picturesque tree-lined canals. I feel at ease in this busy metropolis, with its friendly and relaxed atmosphere. Even though I'm a stranger, I feel welcome in this city which doesn't judge, and which permits me to be free to experiment in self-discovery. I accept the open invitation to enjoy all of its charm and beauty. I cannot help but admire the tall old narrow buildings that lean at odd-angles, and the beautiful boats, which line the canals. Compared to what I'm used to, there are not many cars here, at least not in this area. I see plenty of people riding bicycles, traveling on the tourist canal cruises or on the frequently passing trams. I love the culture and the difference. There are lots of pedestrians wandering the city. Happiness rules the air. Maybe it's due to the liberal attitudes towards marijuana and sex, but people seem happy, and laughter fills the streets and alleyways.

There is a large statue of the famous Dutch painter Rembrandt in the center of the square, from whom the area is named, atop a gray granite plinth bearing his signature. We take a side street and arrive at a strip club with bright neon signs outside, illuminating its existence. It doesn't look like any kind of club that I've been to before. I see a number of people with warm smiles on their faces ready to welcome us in for a good time. Nickolaus greets a large black doorman, and I get the feeling he's been here before, as he speaks easily with him. We enter the club and a regular looking middle-aged woman, and a sexy brunette with bright red lipstick approaches us. She smiles at me and comes close enough that I can smell her perfume. Nickolaus winks at me.

"Don't worry. Relax. It will be fun."

I look around and everything is new territory for me, from the red neon mood lighting to the music playing. We enter a small room with dancing poles and wall to wall mirrors, and immediately the bell goes off in my head.

The brunette hands me a glass of champagne. I take a few sips and the bubbles welcome me. I drink more, knowing that I'm going to need some Dutch courage.

Now topless, this sexy girl approaches the pole and begins performing a sexual dance of amazing athleticism. Her partner is the pole. Her talent, strength and beauty mesmerize me.

She moves her body effortlessly up and down the vertical burlesque pole, like a cat on the prowl. Every inch of her is fit, from her firm arms to her thighs and gorgeous voluptuous butt. I'm enjoying watching this spectacle of dance moves and maneuvers and the contours of her body hugging the pole. Her athletic body moves slowly and the ripples of her muscles change shape with her direction. Her core strength is dynamic as she spreads her legs around the pole and moves in a circular spin. Moving her hips in and out even gets me excited, as I watch the self-expression of her confidence, grace, strength, fitness, and breathtaking acrobatic movement all rolled into one sexually charged performance. Her movements flow in an entrancing rhythmic dance. Watching her twisting and twirling around the pole, I find myself eager to have a go. Inching up and down the pole, she wraps her left leg around it, while gracefully moving around it, in her stiletto heels, in a sexy manner.

She leans backwards, her long hair falling parallel with the pole, while comfortably clinging to it with her muscular thighs. Swiveling her hips she makes any firefighter look like a novice. The sexy brunette, now horizontal with the pole, quickly moves to a split on the floor. Her arms wave and dance around it like she's worshiping a goddess. Another glass of champagne should do the trick and I'm golden to participate. My eyes are begging for more and the only way I know it will keep going is if I physically show an interest. No one notices a participant on the sidelines. I want to seduce the pole like I've just witnessed. To be great at sex you need a good willing partner, and I'm going to step right up to imitate my master.

I step forward onto the stage, grab the pole and start to tease it with my motivated hips. I close my eyes, allowing the music to fill my ears, and let the natural rhythm of my body take control. I'm in a trance. My black skirt sways back and forth, as I slide and gyrate my hips like I want to make love to the pole. Fixating on moving sensually and sexually, I aim to please those who may be watching. I slowly peel off my red top to reveal my black lace bra. I wriggle and wiggle my body up and down as I pretend to lick the pole, like it's a tasty cock that I want to give a good blowjob. My moves mimic those of a porn star as confidence fills me and I take to the pole full throttle. With one sweeping motion, I remove my skirt to reveal my matching lace panties. I move up and down, licking my lips, like I've just felt the best ever orgasm between my legs. Trying not to moan too loud, I'm feeling the rhythm in a slow sexual motion. I see out of the corner of my eye that my sensual moves are driving Nickolaus crazy as he smiles in pleasure. With his nodding and smiling approval, I unhook my bra, dropping it to the floor, revealing my large breasts and erect nipples. He has his hands in his pants and I can see the movement in his jeans as he firmly grips and strokes his hard cock. His eyes are smoldering and he has a big smile. I know that he's in the zone and feeling it.

The room temperature is rising due to the fire and heat that my hips are producing. I move and shake my big ass up and down, working the pole. It doesn't matter what my size is because all eyes will be on my tits, my ass, my show, and me. The voyeur's visual pleasure is my ultimate aim and reward. I relate to the pole like it's the best damn sexual partner I've ever had, and I aim to please. I trace my fingers along the pole, then seductively put my fingers to my mouth and suck on my fingertips. I close my eyes and slowly run my fingers down my body, heading south towards my hot wet pussy. In this moment of unadulterated exhibitionism I am so fucking turned on.

I slide my hand down into my panties, grabbing my pussy and touching my clit. I insert my finger in and out, feeling the warmth of my juices. It feels so good! The pleasure feels so damn hot as I think of Nickolaus. His cock doesn't let me down, as it stands tall and proud. I glance towards him and see that he's enjoying my performance. He asks nothing of me and I imagine that any paying voyeurs will just want more. Moves that I didn't know I could do are being created as I continue to explore every inch of the pole. Each move is spontaneous and flows like a natural love-making session between two old lovers who know the maps of each other's bodies.

Nickolaus' smile and bright eyes are following my every move. The hot red-lipped brunette approaches and moves her hips behind me, grinding really close. Feeling her sweat and desire, I'm not sure what turns me on more, her pussy swaying and touching my firm ass or the excited look from Nickolaus as he watches. I continue my moves and follow her lead. This public sexual spectacle is open to be viewed by anyone who happens to be passing by. Red Lips rubs her hand gently down my neck and around my shoulders and upper back, while moving closer and kissing me from my ear down to my neck. She's sexier than the Pussycat

Dolls and I find myself attracted to her dominating attention.

She grabs my hair with her fist and pulling it back, draws me towards her and whispers in my ear, "That was such a fucking hot show that you just gave."

I turn around and stare deeply into her brown eyes. Our eyes stick like glue, and I'm suddenly oblivious to my surroundings. It's like there is no one but the two of us in the room. I'm transfixed by her scent, close proximity and beauty. She opens her mouth with protruding lips and presses them firmly against mine. They cling to me and we kiss passionately, opening and closing our mouths as we mimic and mirror one another. She pushes her tongue into my mouth, and I reciprocate, our tongues dancing together in frenzied desire. I close my eyes to increase the intensity of this pleasure. Her hands run down from my shoulders, caressing my curves, as they head towards and tightly grab my ass. Our pussies connect, rubbing against each other. Red Lips starts kissing my cheek, then moving down the front of my neck, to the top of my chest until she reaches my breasts. She grabs me with her teasing fingers. My eyes follow her and I succumb to her kissing my breasts and sucking on my nipple, while moving her hands between my thighs. My pussy is getting wet and red as I pulsate my hips closer to her hands, gyrating and rubbing myself onto her rigid thumb.

She plays me like her favorite instrument. She moves her head further down, kissing my belly and rolling her tongue in a circular motion.

She lifts her head and looks up, then rises, grabs the back of my neck and whispers in my ear, "I love your sexy style mama."

I kiss her forcefully and insert my tongue into her willing mouth. Gyrating her hips with mine, I stretch and move to her rhythms.

I push my body slowly and firmly against hers and whisper in her ear, "Show me what you can do. I want to pleasure you like you have never been pleasured before. All your past experiences were just practice for me."

I go one step further, sliding my hand into her red silk panties and deliberately finger her pussy. She moans with delight as I flick my fingers faster with relentless passion. Then, I grab her breast and lower my head. I look at her seductively and force her hard nipple into my mouth, licking, sucking and gently nibbling it. She bites her bottom lip in pleasure and I am the dominator now. I open up my legs and hug her upper thigh with them. She responds wildly by shoving her hand into my panties and fingering my vagina. Ooh, it feels so fucking good! Her thin fingers immediately feel my hot juice dripping onto them. I'm panting and feeling the heat rise between us. This delicious process is as wild as fuck. I kiss the top of her sweating shoulder, and then suck on her bottom lip. She cups my ass with her hands and grinds me firmly. I play with and twist her erect pink nipples. Kissing and sucking her neck, I pet her hair like she's a good kitty cat. Our eyes meet again and I stick my tongue out at her and lick my lips in a provocative fashion. She takes her fingers out of my pussy and licks and sucks on them.

"The taste of pure American honey is something to be savored!"

We lie down on the stage and she climbs on top of me like a cat on the prowl. She's more erotic than a hard cock. Each stroke and lick that she gives me has me wanting more.

"I'm hungry. Give me that sweet fucking pussy of yours!" she commands.

I'm incredibly horny as she slips off my wet panties. This sexy mama wants it bad, like I've never wanted to experience anything before. Red Lips is hot, with her sweet flesh looking mighty fine. Her yummy salty flesh tastes good on my lips. I'm about to blow as I push my breasts forward and thrust my hips towards her. There are no chances here, because I know she wants me, as her eyes reveal her lust for my loins. She takes her long pink tongue and licking hard and fast, tastes the juices of my pussy. She plunges her tongue deeper and deeper inside me. I can feel the tip of her tongue moving at a rapid pace, and her oral stimulation makes my juices flow uncontrollably. Our movements are fast as we twist in every direction. I shudder and open my legs wider for her to gain full access. She takes her fingers and rapidly stimulates my clitoris. I grab my breasts to trigger more pleasures and begin to moan. I take deeper breaths and am feeling hot. She clenches my ass and gives it a big slap. Ooh that hurt, but feels so damn good!

"You dirty, dirty girl! You want more?" she says while catching her breath.

I moan louder and tilt my head back. My vagina expands and lengthens like an automatic biological reaction to let her fully in. She tongues me some more and my breathing becomes heavier. I feel a sweet rush of intense juices and orgasm coming. I tremble and my hips move in a circular motion to push her deeper inside me. She sucks my flesh and nibbles at my fold. She moves her mouth all around delicately and firmly at the same time. She starts to finger me too, giving me double the sensation. Ooh that feels so damn crazy and the creamy hot orgasm flows as my body trembles. She holds me close and gentle. My first experience being eaten out by a woman feels out of this world. I'm curious to find out what her pussy tastes like.

As if she's just read my mind, she opens her legs wide.

"You want to taste something creamy and sweet?"

Nodding my head, I get down on my knees and begin by kissing her inner thighs. She arches her back and I move my mouth to her clitoris, licking it up and down as quickly as I can. Her honey sweet taste is such a turn on. Gazing upwards I can see her eyes close and I know that I'm hitting the right spots. I lick her again and again with each hard pulsating move, trying to give her whole body pleasure with my one sensual tongue. Her muscles spasm and tense all at once. She grabs my head and forces it hard against her pussy. Red Lips moves me in the direction of her pleasures, grinding her hot wet pussy against my mouth. She bends her legs and rests her calves on my back. I finger her G-spot with sweet intensity, while alternating between licking and sucking on her sweet juices. Her moans encourage me to explore and pleasure her further. I change positions, opening her legs and climbing on top of her, locking our clitorises in a scissor position. It makes her pussy drip with excitement. Her bright red vagina swells with anticipation as she enjoys feeling my wet pussy against hers. As I gaze into her sparkling eyes, she puts her hand around my waist, holding me tightly against her. We mash our clits and lips together in a sexual dance. Grinding our crotches in sexual frenzy. She moans louder and louder as her eyes close in pure pleasure. My honey hole is wet and tingling. I want to give her the best damn thigh tingling orgasm she's ever reached. Desire, yearning, and passion are bringing me to my sexual intoxication. I'm mesmerized by her moves and abilities. A mixture of sweat and sex fills the air. I struggle to catch my breath as I concentrate hard on my every move to get her to orgasm.

"Yes, yes, ooh yes!"

She cries out, "Ahh, ahh!"

Red Lips arches her back and her hot creamy cum trickles out. Her body is glistening with the warm glow of sex. Our pussy locking exercise has her fulfilled. Sloppy, wet pussy juice is all over our thighs and the floor. Her sultry brown eyes dilate. I cradle her head on my chest to comfort and relax her even more. She kisses my neck and we lie there in each other's arms.

Smiling at her and running my fingers through my sexed up hair, I say, "Thanks for being my first!"

She kisses me back and spoons me close. Her arms and legs wrap around me like a nice warm human blanket.

"I could never tell. You have natural instinct. It's like you unleashed something inside you that was wanting to come out all along."

She nuzzles against my neck and I feel content. Her words validate that what we've just experienced is not dirty, or wrong. I pushed my boundaries, was allowed to explore my sexuality, indulge my curiosity and was accepted by another human being, whose heart beats just like mine. I offered myself to her and was warmly welcomed. It was more than just exchanging enchanting pleasantries. We connected deeply on a physical and primal level. Pure intimacy and acceptance all rolled into one. I surprised myself with my own performance and indulgence.

Oh what joyful pleasure!

Nickolaus stares at us from above, his cock still fully erect. In my excitement I had momentarily forgotten all about his presence. He smiles at me, like a boy who has just scored a home run on opening day with the cheers of his home crowd supporting him.

"I see you have taken in some of the deep pleasures of Amsterdam. It suits you Sam."

He gives me a wink of approval, bends over and kisses me on the cheek in a sexual way.

While I've thoroughly enjoyed exploring and challenging my sexual barriers and boundaries with Red Lips, he's the one that I've started to form an emotional connection with during our short time together.

"How about we get some rest before we discover more of Amsterdam?"

He takes my hand and I follow him, although I find it hard to leave the warm and comforting arms of Red Lips. She blows me a kiss goodbye, as she's probably done many times to many casual sexual partners in her life. I smile and mouth "thank you" back. I gather up my discarded garments, re-dress, and moments later I leave this enchanting fantasy room, and we find ourselves once again on the streets of Amsterdam.

Nickolaus knows his way around like it's his second home. He's my tour guide and I dreamily follow. I stare once again at the architecture, rolling clouds and narrow streets. He books us into a small hotel for the night, and once settled in our room, I fall blissfully asleep in my relaxed state.

~ Recipe 7 ~
Crossing The Line

Prep time:	One
Serves:	One too many

This recipe is not for the faint-hearted. It will challenge one to explore in ways never imagined. The magnitude of the ingredients can be overpowering. There is no harm in experimenting to create the right atmosphere.

Creativity:	Different sex positions
Cost:	Receive extra money
Culinary:	Eat cream
Culture:	Participate in brothel
Connect:	Experience multiple partners

The creamy vanilla curtains, fringed with lace and a darker beige pattern decorate the window perfectly. Left ajar, they allow sunlight to enter the room.

I open my eyes wide to see sunshine hitting the middle of the parquet wooden floor, as if frozen in time. The sun's rays make me think of God, and I consider why I've not prayed to Him for a while.

It's not because I haven't wanted to, but I've been so wrapped up in myself that I haven't had too many thoughts about prayer, and when I did have an opportunity in Cologne, a couple of days ago, I couldn't find the right words. Besides, at the moment what do I have to pray about? No one in my life is suffering from a bout of cancer. I'm not faced with taking an important exam. My brother hasn't been involved in a terrible car crash. The weatherman isn't calling for a huge snowstorm, leaving me needing to rush out before it hits to buy my weekly supply of milk, bread, eggs and other groceries. Can I pray about such insignificant things to the creator of the universe?

Is it better to pray while in a group environment? Should I pray harder when I'm weak, afraid and alone? Will my prayers be better heard if I pray in a church, instead of this hotel room?

But, what do I really need to pray and ask God's help for? Should I start praying for a new job or unexpected wealth? For those that are dying? For the President to make a right decision? Or, should I pray just for the sake of praying, like the prayers I used to say when I was a little girl before I went to bed, because my mom told me to.

Why do some people pray more than others? Is it because their faith tells them to, or has it become habit, like reciting the Pledge of Allegiance? Memorized words repeated automatically by children all across the country each morning. The words, purely an affirmation of a belief system. Do they really mean anything, and will speaking them out loud make a difference?

How much should I pray? If I don't pray enough, does that mean I'll fall out of God's favor? If I pray more, will each additional prayer result in more help and less suffering? Should I tell more people that I'm praying, and will that make a difference? Will it help me to become a stronger person, better able to avoid any temptations put in my way? Should I keep asking until I get what I want?

Why does God let good people suffer? Will He judge me on all the things I've done wrong, and how will I know if I've done wrong in His eyes? Should I assuage my guilty feelings by confessing everything, just in case? Will Karma make a difference? If I make a larger donation to the church, will that increase the chances of my prayer being heard, and of me being forgiven?

What is the real purpose of prayer? Is it to comfort, ask for guidance, a cry for help, or for when I'm really fucked and don't know where else to turn?

Why are there so many different religions, and who is to say which God is the right one to pray to? Why do I pray anyway? Have I lost my religion and if so, when and where did it go?

So many questions!

Lyrics to the song "Losing my Religion" by R.E.M. enter my head.

I wish there was someone to help guide me through all these thoughts. Perhaps I will take up wishing instead. I wonder whether Nickolaus prays, and if so, how often. I don't even know if he's religious, or atheist for that matter. We've not discussed religion in our short time together. We just accept each other as we are and are enjoying each other's company. He certainly seems to have a strong free will, and appears very accepting of life. I'm sure his God would love him no matter what.

We lay under the sheets nestled in each other's arms, shifting slightly to find the right position to be comfortable. I'm becoming deeply connected to him and not feeling threatened. Nickolaus snores, but that's OK. It isn't irritating, it's actually quite comforting, because I know that he's as relaxed as I am. It feels good to just rest and not need to rush to be anywhere. We are our own timekeepers. I could get used to this pace of life. Nickolaus rolls over, opens his eyes and looks at me in a different way than he's done before.

"You are one interesting sexy girl," he says, while running his fingers through my hair and staring deeply into my baby blues.

I find it hard to be considered sexy, when for most of my life I was never given a second look. I look down at my body, disbelief still an automatic reaction. He lifts my chin up with the tips of his fingers, and makes direct eye contact again.

"Yes, you silly thing. It's all inside you and now I see it coming out. Believe that it's true."

"I could start to believe in anything you say. You could make anyone believe."

I wrap my body around him like I'm his blanket. I love all of his physical displays of affection. I crave it and feel like a spoiled child. After years of misery and feelings of isolation, I'm in overdrive. He makes me feel younger with all the sexual energy that he focuses on me. I've never felt this vibrant and joyful before. He's awoken my senses and makes me feel full of life. The feeling is amazing and has me yearning for more.

"Sam, you really turn me on!"

Before he finishes his sentence, I can feel his firm pleasure stick getting harder, pressing against my thigh.

"I want you to get a hold of it and stroke it for me."

His commands are simple. I've never really given much thought to giving a hand job. It seems so ninth grade, and most bad girls would presumably prefer to give a good old-fashioned blowjob. I stare at and start stroking his large firm cock. Feeling its warmth in my hand starts to get my pussy wet. I spit on my palm and rub it onto his cock to give it instant lubrication to get the job started. I try to find the pleasure points that will excite and arouse him. Placing my left hand with my thumb on his inner shaft and my pointer and middle finger on the outer, I slowly and firmly massage his corona and frenulum. I look at him seductively, licking my lips in a suggestive manner and know that he's enjoying my moves. Wrapping both hands around his manhood I firmly move them rhythmically, and he begins to moan.

Twisting both hands in opposite directions, he lies back giving me total control and access, while continuing to groan in delight. When my hand reaches the top of his penis, I swivel and cup the head completely with my wet palm, simulating a warm vagina.

I keep repeating this motion, massaging with my left hand while using a V-shaped finger technique along his firm cock with my right.

I encircle his penis with my thumb and forefinger. My grip is firm but relaxed. I wonder what the sensations I'm giving to him feel like, and whether it's comparable to the feelings I have when I play with myself. Is this what penis envy is all about? I increase the speed and rhythm, as he's so into it. As I gently rub the coronal ridge at the back of the head of his penis, he arches his back. The action is all in the wrist and not just the hands. My movements are flowing with ease. It's like a royal wave to give his penis a good ending. Making a loose fist with one hand, I slide it up to the top of Nickolaus' penis. He grabs my head, and rubs my hair. Reaching his penis head, I finish with a little twist. Gently gliding and moving up, I hold his penis hostage for a moment. Then, I move my free hand lower and play with his crown jewels, cupping and gently massaging his balls. I can sense my moves are driving him wild.

"You like?" I ask with a hot smile.

"Oh Sam, you are good. So damn good!" he says, lying on his back in a pleasurable state of bliss.

His stiffened member is responding in ecstasy to my rhythm. At this point, he's at my mercy and my command. I keep my hand close to his tip and play with it slowly. I make a circle with my first and middle finger on the top of the scrotum. From the bottom to the top, I move my hands over and over again. Interlacing the thin fingers of both hands, I create a one-sided tunnel. Pumping rhythmically up and down, I make him squirm. Circling with my thumbs, I place the tunnel over his erect penis and run it up and down. I decide to tease him a little and play with his balls as I pull up on his shaft with my other hand. He's enjoying my dominance and is moaning with pleasure. Caressing and manipulating his penis is sending chills down his spine as he grinds himself into my hands and moans even louder. I touch and caress every part of his genitalia, and gently massage his perineum. I can see by the way that he's grinding and moving his hips that his raging hard-on is about to explode.

He grabs my head and says, "Open your mouth wide. I want you to taste me!"

I rest my head on his stomach, open my mouth and close my eyes briefly. I've never tasted a man's orgasmic juices before. I can sense he's ready to cum for me. I can see the rush of excitement, as the blood heats and reddens the tip of his penis. He moans loudly and his body tenses and quivers uncontrollably as his cock explodes, the ejaculation of hot sperm spurting out and landing on my cheek. I stick out my tongue to catch and taste some. His hot salty cum explodes, everywhere. He shoots out more of his load, some into my mouth and down my face. I've pleased him with my actions and response.

He reaches for his cock and massages it slowly and firmly, emptying the last drops of his pleasure, and then grabs me close and holds me tightly. We are like two hot blankets of sexual heat. I've tasted his salty pleasure, another first for me. This is a raw and an intimate feeling. Gently, I wipe away his cum from my face with a nearby t-shirt. Nickolaus is happily staring at me like I've just made the Olympic team. Once again, I'm feeling relaxed and satisfied. There is no one present to judge me on my actions. My boundaries have been challenged and extended.

"Sam, you surprise me with your willingness and free spirit. I would never have guessed that you were so good."

I lean towards him and rest my head on his shoulder.

"It's thanks to you. Without you I would have never known that I was capable of such things. You are the one that tempts me to experience these pleasures. You inspire me! I am breaking free and I am in your light."

In that moment I recollect The Who singing "See Me, Feel Me." The words of the song from Tommy resonate strongly right now. My body glows, as I'm no longer in denial of my newly found sexuality. Being with Nickolaus, I get excitement from head to toe. Looking out of the window I see rain falling with a splitter splatter onto the cobblestone street below. My will has been tested many times in my life. I realize that I've been away from my kids and father for over a week. I think about calling them but Nickolaus interrupts me from my thoughts. Right now, my adventures are my priority no matter what the cost.

"Sam, before we head back to Cologne I thought we would try something even more adventurous later today, if you're interested. You can be part of it or be on the sidelines if you wish."

He grabs me from behind with a hard but gentle squeeze and kisses my neck.

I'm so vulnerable around him and he has me curious and absolutely mesmerized. Amsterdam is known for Van Gogh, Rembrandt, museums, canals, bicycles, and pretty tulips.

"As long as it's legal right?" I say, giving him a mischievous grin.

Where else is there a law that states that you don't need to wear a helmet but you are required to have a light and a bell on your bike?

We clean ourselves up, get dressed, gather our belongings and head out.

We walk alongside canals, with their still waters reflecting the soft morning light, without a care in the world. I find the peacefulness of the area so relaxing. The rain is light but there is no need for an umbrella, as we wander hand in hand, down narrow tree-lined streets. With Nickolaus, the sun is shining in my heart and throughout my world. I'm so happy that I could sing "Singing in the Rain," like Gene Kelly, because I'm on such a high, and there are no gray clouds in my life. We exchange playful glances and smiles, sidestepping and dodging puddles along the way. We arrive at a café, with a brightly graffitied exterior. Like a true gentleman, Nickolaus holds open the door and we enter. He orders some coffee and space cakes. I find it ironic that the café is right next door to a police station.

"Hey, this will be better than you coughing for fifteen minutes," he laughs, remembering my first experience with him, "and it's legal, cheap and quite delicious," he says as he willingly shares his treats.

He doesn't have to give any special code or hand gesture to obtain them, he just openly orders them and pays his money. I find it strange that what is considered illegal and would get me into trouble in the States is considered normal, acceptable, and legal here. How liberating! I am enjoying the freedom that this city affords. We find a nice comfy couch to chill and indulge. The back room offers a great view of the canal, and many passing tourists. The big open bay windows allowing smoke to escape, and letting fresh air in. The sound of acid jazz fills the air as we enjoy our cake and each other's company. Slowly the effect of the cake starts to kick in. I'm feeling warm and fuzzy inside. One minute I'm in the middle of an important speech on thoughtful subjects, the next my mind goes blank, to the point where I end up asking Nickolaus to remind me what I was talking about. He doesn't remember, and we both giggle hysterically. Relaxing on the couch I close my eyes and see colored lights dancing all around me, stimulated and influenced by the sound of the drum rhythms, synthesizers and brass melodies. Wow, this is so fucking cool! This altered state of perception is giving me an experience I couldn't possibly imagine with my normal state of mind. The music changes and suddenly my brain is processing the sound of euphoric uplifting trance music. I'm in a dream state, watching a psychedelic light show being projected onto the inside of my eyelids. Hell, yeah!

I feel a tap on my shoulder, and opening my eyes I'm suddenly back in the café with Nickolaus stood over me.

"Are you ready to move on?" he asks.

We leave the room and the music, and walk around the city, going from one place to another. It's like I'm awake in a dream. I'm like Alice wandering around Wonderland. Everything is so bright, colorful, exciting and ever so slightly off kilter. I'm awake, dreaming that I'm dreaming that I'm awake. Curiouser and curiouser said Sammie, as she walked dreamily through dreamy Amsterdam. It does seem like this trip is taking an eternity. When we finally arrive I can barely remember what we just did, or how we got there. It feels like we arrived almost instantly. Maybe this is what the space cake is all about because it all feels relaxing and pleasurable, and, well different. I'm so carefree and living in the moment. Nickolaus takes my hand and guides me to a club in the red light district with a gleam in his eyes like I haven't seen before. He's acting like a little schoolboy full of eager anticipation.

"I want this for you. To experience multiple pleasures."

Nickolaus looks at me with a twinkle in his eye, as we approach a curvaceous girl with Angelina Jolie lips. He smiles, greets and hugs her, and they converse in Dutch. Their genuine exchange of pleasantries appears to be a usual occurrence. I don't know what they are saying but I smile as they giggle together. I find it hard not to be jealous of their little flirtatious exchanges.

The history they have together is evident. It's something that I'll never have with Nickolaus and I find myself feeling unexpectedly annoyed at myself for feeling this way. Nickolaus doesn't seem bothered about my feelings and moves straight in on his own agenda. Curves takes us to a room where another couple are already laying naked on a bed, in a sixty-nine position, eating each other like animals. My eyes open wide as this is completely new territory for me, witnessing a couple of naked strangers performing oral sex on each other. Their moans and enjoyment are apparent as Long Legs moves to suck Muscles' cock. Nickolaus starts taking his clothes off and looks at me seductively. He takes control over me, and starts removing my clothes. I stand frozen for a moment, like a deer in the headlights, not knowing where to turn. Muscles moves towards me, and with his firm fingers begins gently stimulating my nipples to relax me. Long Legs gets down on her knees, wraps her forearms around my hips, grabbing my ass, and immediately starts licking my pussy. Their pace is rapid, taking my breath away as I get caught up in this immediate pleasure. Nickolaus starts massaging my shoulders at the same time. I'm feeling pleasure from every direction. The surge of rubbing and licking makes me wet and surprisingly horny. My senses are on overdrive as every piece of me is feeling aroused. Muscles grabs my hair, holding my head firmly with his hand, and passionately kisses my neck. He then bends me over and sticks his hot hard cock deep inside me. There is no foreplay involved. I grab whatever piece of flesh that I can hold onto, resting my hands on Curves shoulders, as she's still on her knees in front of me. I can see excitement in her eyes, knowing that I'm a fresh face to this arrangement. She responds by raising her head and French kissing me, shoving her tongue in my mouth, licking and sucking on mine. Nickolaus is very excited, gripping firmly onto his rock hard cock which is standing firm and proud. Witnessing two girls kissing must be a turn on for him, and we are pleasing him with our display. Muscles, who has been pumping his cock deep inside my wet pussy pulls out and moves it to my ass, gently sliding into me from behind.

I'm startled at first and cry out as this new experience hurts. My parts weren't made for his long thick cock. I sense his excitement at my virgin experience, as my tight ass grips firmly to his throbbing cock. He thrusts his pelvis back and forth against me. Curves fondles my breasts and takes turns licking and sucking on my erect nipples. The animal scents in the room are magnified by the moans that accompany them. Muscles moves me to a bed in the middle of the room and lays me down on my back. He spreads my legs wide open and quickly shoves his cock inside me in the missionary position. Nickolaus at the same time moves his cock to my mouth. He closes his eyes in intense pleasure, as I put his whole cock in my mouth and suck it real hard. Long Legs starts touching and rubbing Nickolaus' ass to get his attention. She moves around him, brushing her body against his, and begins kissing him. I forget all my pleasures momentarily and watch intently. He's kissing her back, and taking his cock out of my mouth, moves her closer. He lays her down and jumps on top of her, shoving his cock deep inside her. He puts his hands under her ass and grinds her hard and fast. She moans loudly with pleasure. While this is happening I'm just fixated on his obvious enjoyment. I watch as he gets excited to the point of orgasm and pulls out right before showering her tummy with his abundant cum. Their eyes connect, two hearts beating as one, and I suddenly feel like an elephant in the room.

Muscles moves me around like a rag doll, taking me in multiple positions. I move wherever he puts me, but I feel nothing. I'm like a robot, just there to let him get off. I can't help but keep staring at Nickolaus and Long Legs. Is it jealousy that I'm feeling? Surely, that's a silly thought. I don't own or control Nickolaus. Why do I resent the fact that he fucked Long Legs and not me? Have I become far more attached to him than I thought? Maybe I'm beyond having a man with no deep feelings for me, or a friend with benefits. Feelings of hurt and betrayal are sticking to me. Am I wrong for feeling that way? Am I being misled by my own perceptions? It's not like we even discussed things or are exclusive.

Our relationship has never been defined, so why do I feel like it's threatened and jeopardized? I realize that I've become emotionally attached to this man for teaching me new freedoms. He accepts me as I am and I love these feelings, but the dynamics are changing now. Who is to blame? I got caught up in the fun moments of expression. I need to leave to collect my thoughts. I'm no longer on the high that I was on before.

I look down at the floor and my chin hits the ground. Disentangling myself from Muscles, I gather my belongings and start to dress as quickly as I can. Long Legs and Nickolaus are lying there together in post-orgasm ecstasy. I can't take it any longer and try to leave the room, but before I do so, Muscles takes something out of his jacket pocket, and hands it to me. A handful of euro notes.

He laughs and says, "That was a real good fuck, my sweet luscious American. I hope we can do it again sometime soon."

He winks at me. I look away. I can't continue to make eye contact with him.

Did he just pay me for the sex that we experienced? I take the money and leave the room as quickly as I can. I feel dirty and disgusted.

Trying to process all that has just happened, I feel ashamed and low. I'm not a prostitute but I feel like a giant whore. What did I get myself into? Did I go too far in my quest to discover myself? Was it pure pleasure that I was looking for? I had forgotten who I was and my purpose. I've been fooling myself. I haven't been fully satisfied with my life and allowed my desires and impulses to take control. I've become corrupted and easily swayed. I've sinned badly. Where is my faith now? I will be judged by my actions. The church has a strong influence over me but in the moment I forgot all of that. I don't love or respect myself right now. Will I be misunderstood for the wrong decisions I've made? I've a lot to confess for the sins that I've done and witnessed. How will I ever make it right to my God and myself? My mind is racing and I'm mentally torturing myself in my own private hell.

My hedonistic pleasures and desires would have made the Cyrenaics proud. The Greeks knew of hedonism, and were taught that the only intrinsic good is pleasure, which meant not just the absence of pain, but to positively enjoy sensations. For centuries, people have been tempted by pleasure, but how much is too much and where are my own boundaries? If it's legal is it OK to experience? I certainly experienced a lot of enjoyable sensations, but what sacrifices have I made, and who have I hurt in the process? In the moment, I depersonalized myself and felt nothing from my head or heart. In the end, I merely went through the motions, not thinking about what it all meant. The feelings were momentary and I kept wanting more. I did not make a distinction to my past or present life. They were separate entities. My momentary sexual pleasures were very physical ones. I'm at the end of my rope and just left to hang my own soul.

The old Babylonian version of the "Epic of Gilgamesh" talks about Siduri's advice, which was to eat, drink and be merry. In my moment of dancing I forgot about the realism of responsibility. I received a lot of bodily pleasures that were intense but fleeting.

The song by George Michael, "Faith," with its Bo Diddley beat and classic rock and roll rhythm fills my head. Music has always provided me with a calm reminder of how to think about myself in times of trouble. It's my escape and emotional release. My raw feelings give me a great deal of shame, for doing wrong in God's eyes. I'm no longer impulsive and thinking solely of my pleasures. In the end, my God will judge me for what I've done. Can I live with these thoughts of judgment? I am full of shame and remorse, but I cannot change what has happened, only what I will do in the future in order to conquer my demons.

A few moments later Nickolaus exits the room, and sensing my disappointment and disapproval, we head for the train back to Cologne, with barely a word spoken.

~ Recipe 8 ~
Returning To My Roots

Prep time: Seven days
Serves: Family

This recipe will inspire a return back to home. It uses the core ingredients for a life which can sometimes be taken for granted but is always there. It is important not to be too distracted and to focus on the basic elements of the recipe. I will have a deeper appreciation of life as I go through this powerful recipe.

Creativity: Pray
Cost: Lose something valuable
Culinary: Homemade food
Culture: America
Connect: Family

Ring ring. Ring ring. God, will someone answer the phone?

"Hello?"

The voice on the other end of the line sounds distant and weak. Not the normal bold voice I'm used to hearing.

"Hello, Daddy it's me."

There is a silence, which continues for the longest time. I'm not sure if it's because he's realized it's me, and after our last exchange, it's hard for him to pick up from where we left off. My intuition is telling me that something else is going on.

"Daddy, I've so much to talk to you about."

Still silence, but I can hear labored breathing. Cough, cough.

"Man, winter is getting tough around here," says my dad, gasping for the words.

What? No lectures, accusations or me being made to feel bad? Something is definitely wrong! My heart begins to race and my mind wanders. I can't help but think that the worst is yet to come. My internal red flags are starting to give me cause for concern. I can sense that something is wrong, even though I'm miles away from home.

"Dad I need to see you, but I need some help."

There I've admitted it and now I wait for his lecture and judgment. There is another long silent pause.

Cough, cough. More heavy breathing.

"I know. It will be alright, Sammie. It's going to be alright."

Dad acknowledges my offer but something isn't right and I know it.

"Just do one thing for me."

This ghostly conversation seems surreal, like we are on another level and talking about something else, but I just don't get it at the time.

"Whatever, you need Dad. Say it and I'll be there."

Once again in my life there is an eerie quiet silence in facing the realization of my life. But this time I know where I must turn.

Cough, cough.

"You need to love yourself Sammie, and come home to your family where you belong. I can't talk anymore."

His voice is fragile. I've never heard my dad so weak.

"Bye-bye Sammie."

I hang up the phone but I'm left with so many questions running through my head. I'm so far away from home, but feel an urgent need to return immediately. I phone Maria.

"Hey Maria!"

"Hola Sammie! What's all this I'm hearing about you quitting your job. I was wondering why I'd not seen you at work lately. Are these rumors true?"

"Yes. Dawn was really pissing me off and winding me up, so I told the cow what she could do with her job."

"Oh dear! I'm so sorry to hear that," she worriedly responds.

"Don't worry, I'll be OK," I reply.

I'm not sure that I will be, but I say it anyway, hoping it will ring true and be believable.

"What are you up to now?" she asks.

"Believe it or not, I'm actually in Germany right now, but I really need your help Maria."

After giving her a brief summary of my conversation with Dad, Maria bails me out by arranging the next flight home for me from Düsseldorf to John F Kennedy Airport, flying with a bargain airline. It won't be the same experience as flying first class to New Orleans, but the plane will get me to where I need to be. I really do have a good friend that I can count on. I have someone who will always be there for me and guide me in the right direction. Sometimes it's easy to overlook the friendships that matter the most, but at the end of the day, they come through and guide us in our time of need.

I'm always in a rush to wait. I aim to be the one to claim firsties in my row. I find it amusing to hurry up and grab my seat, and then end up waiting the longest for the plane to take off. It must be an impatience thing because I can't be satisfied. I make my way to 33E, all the way towards the back and a middle seat. I quickly put my cabin bag in the overhead storage and sit down before the flight attendant starts making her announcements. More or less every seat is taken, with little room to move for the seven hour and fifty minute journey. I realize that I don't have a cell phone or laptop to shield me from any predators trying to make eye contact. "Howdy ma'am! Nice to meet you!" he says, taking the seat next to me.

I glance to the left to see my travel companion, who reminds me of the country and western singer, Billy Sheen. He looks gorgeous with manicured facial stubble and brown wavy hair falling to his shoulders, underneath a ten-gallon black cowboy hat. On his feet, two-tone black python snakeskin boots. He certainly strikes a favorable first impression.

My mind drifts that maybe after sitting next him for a few hours I should join his fan club, as he's definitely worth checking out.

So, I'm now officially a ma'am. I must appear old to a man his age, or is he just being polite? Why am I being so defensive? Is it my northeast ways coming back to me? I'm conditioned to question. Maria always jokes that I sound like a journalist with all my questions. It's my natural tendency to be curious and want to know more about the world around me. People fascinate me, and I often wonder what motivates them. Why do I act this way with strangers? Well, since I'm stuck here for a long time, I might as well sit back and make the most of it, even though my mind is miles away and still trying to sort itself out.

"Uh. Hi there."

I begin to study his perfect white smile that looks like it's straight out of a television advertisement. I give a quick smile and look down.

"My name is Craig. It's a pleasure to meet you."

His slight facial hair is manly and his brown eyes engaging.

"I'm Samantha."

Short and sweet but I know that this will continue. I look towards him again, and find that I can't stop looking because his facial features are so bold.

"What brings you to Germany? I'm on my way back home to Texas. Looks like I'll still have a long journey ahead of me after this flight arrives in New York."

He looks at me with direct confidence and I know that I won't be able to hide.

I connect with Texas, which allows me to change the focus from my current thoughts.

"What part of Texas? I grew up in Fort Worth, but I haven't been back there since leaving high school."

"That's not too far away. I'm going to Fort Worth for the holidays."

When the plane reaches cruising altitude the flight attendant brings some drinks. Craig orders himself a beer and gets me one as well. The ice is officially broken.

Our conversation begins to flow, informally and without pressure, like we're two old lovers who have so much to catch up on.

The hours pass by and I find myself consumed by his southern accent and charm. His demeanor is genuine and friendly. A few more beers, and I find myself flirting and wearing his hat. I've always thought cowboys were kind of sexy but I know this one is certainly way too young for me. With Craig I find myself asking what there isn't to like about him. He's like a little puppy that you get on Valentine's Day from your sweetheart.

His presence just makes me want to eat him up like my favorite ice cream.

Laughter fills the seats as we connect on so many levels. It's funny that when you share a seat with someone in such a small confined place, you find yourself connecting in intimate ways. Maybe knowing that our paths will never meet again has allowed our walls to come down. My openness to reveal feelings is a ray of light into my heart. I share my horoscope sign of Libra. He chuckles and says that that explains why I seek justice and balance in my life. Then, he pretends to read my palm like he can read my future. He looks at my left palm and says that my fate line indicates that the breaks in it show that I'm prone to many changes in life and direction from external forces. He says that I have a fine hand shape with a rectangular palm and flushed skin. This means that I'm impulsive, spontaneous and do things boldly. It's hard to take him seriously, but inwardly I feel that it rings true. We laugh about the foreign languages we took during high school. I share my stories of taking German and my latest use of the language. Craig tells me that he studied French for a few years, and that his pick-up line is "Voulez-vous coucher avec moi, ce soir?" I giggle and laugh even though I have no clue if he really wants to sleep with me tonight. I know that LaBelle sang Lady Marmalade, even though the Christina Aguilera's version was much more popular than the 1974 version on Soul Train. I didn't even think of that song when I was strutting my stuff in New Orleans.

We talk about embarrassing moments and favorite places that we've traveled to. I even touch on the reasons for my divorce and whether it's easier to live without someone than with them. He tells me that one girlfriend told him that she loved him but could never live with him. Ironically, I wonder why someone would feel that way towards such an engaging person. When someone asks why you got divorced without really knowing you or your ex, it's easy to give a simple matter of fact answer. The truth and reality are of course far more complex, and relationship flaws can take years to unravel. Divorce is such a painful process for all involved. Our conversation makes me think about feelings that I haven't thought about in ages. Craig pays full attention to my stories and interest to the details, which boosts my ego. His genuine smile and honest gestures are the best remedy to help make me feel good about life again.

Our landing is near and I don't want our conversation or connection to finish. It's inevitable in life that all good things must come to an end. Sometimes I'm ready and can anticipate the ending, and at other times it just hits me. I like to be in control of things and find myself lost and overwhelmed when things are out of my control. My direction and balance can become out of kilter and it really throws me off. Adapting to change and surprises are not things that come easily.

"Goodbye pretty lady. It's been a pleasure spending time with you. If you're ever in Fort Worth, or find yourself on Facebook, look me up."

He tilts his hat and smiles, before taking it off and handing it to me.

"I want you to take this."

I'm longer a ma'am, I'm now a pretty lady. I blush at his compliment and gift, feeling confident and ready to face any challenges that come my way. My journey has been wild and I'm ready to go home where I belong. I'm a broken and dysfunctional person filled with baggage, as I learn about my limits and grow with my experiences. Loving and accepting myself is where I need to begin. I need to have faith and trust in that. I can't blame anyone for making me feel bad, or for what they've done to me. I need to be accountable to myself.

I turn to Craig and give him a big hug.

"Thank you for the gift of insight, Craig. You're a true American gentleman. Have a safe trip home."

We grab our bags and head on our separate journeys, separating like opposing headlights passing one another in the deep dark night. If fate allows, our paths may cross again. After being away from home and on many travels, my house feels different. Its architecture doesn't compare to the fabulous buildings I've seen on my journeys. It's very quiet and while familiar it seems strange to be back.

My refrigerator looks like it could house a small army, compared to the ones I've seen in Europe. I see that dust has gathered on the sideboard since it has lain unpolished for so long. Just as I decide that my housework can wait until another time, and that I'm going to jump into a nice hot shower, and then head for my comfy bed, my thoughts are interrupted by a knock at the door. I answer it and am greeted by my dad. He looks somewhat fragile and I immediately stare into his faded blue eyes.

"Oh Dad. I'm so sorry. I've missed you!"

He enters the house and I give him a big hug and a kiss. He gives me a weak hug in return.

"Hi Sammie, we've a lot to catch," cough cough, "up on."

He's short of breath, his breathing labored, the wrinkles on his forehead are pronounced against his pale white skin, and he's also sweating profusely.

"Dad, are you alright?"

A concerned look runs across my face.

"Oh honey, it's probably just heartburn or something."

He puts his hand to his chest and struggles for his words to come out.

"You know that pizza gets me every time, or maybe it's the flu that I'm getting. It's almost like I swallowed a golf ball."

"Dad. Why don't you come over here and take a seat?"

I sense that something isn't right. In a matter of moments the big wide world is suddenly starting to feel very small, and time feels like it's slowing down, as the second hand on the clock seems to take an eternity to move from one position to its next. All that's on my mind is a deep rush of panic.

"Talk to me. What's going on?"

I give him a big side cuddle like we are sitting beside each other on a park bench.

Sweat is beginning to collect on his brow. I take a tissue and gently wipe his forehead like he's an ill child.

"Dad I love you, you know."

I don't know why I rush to say these words. Something comes over me like I have to make peace with the world.

Cough cough. Uggh! My dad grabs his chest and slumps forward with his fists clenched. He tries to rub his chest to relieve the tension. His short labored breaths move from raspy and metallic to almost non-existent. His eyes glaze over and he briefly stares at me.

"I know honey!"

He makes an eerie sound like my old vacuum cleaner used to do, woo, woo. The lights and his pulse seem to be leaving his world. He falls to the floor, seemingly in slow motion, like an onlooker watching an inevitable car crash.

"No! Don't do this! Not now! Dad! Wake up!"

I feel for his pulse, but it's very weak. Stay calm. I can't think! What did I learn when I took my CPR class? Try to relax. OK. Let's breathe. I shout and begin getting angry at his lack of a response.

"Dad, oh Dad. Please stay with me!"

I loosen his clothing, and reach for the phone to call the emergency services.

"I need an ambulance. My father. Francis Martin. I think he's having a heart attack. Age? Seventy-two. OK, thank you. Please tell them to hurry!"

It's difficult for me to see him in so much pain.

"The ambulance is on its way. Do you hear me? Dad wake up!"

Uncontrollable tears run down my face.

My dad is lying in front of me, unconscious and is not breathing normally. He's unresponsive like a china doll. Trying to lay him down flat on the floor, I get annoyed at the clutter in my own house. Why haven't I been home to clean up? Damn it!

"Dad it will be alright. Breathe. Just breathe. I can do CPR."

The air in the room is stifling and I can hardly breathe myself. I feel numb, like this is a dream. Please let me wake up from this horrible nightmare. Let it not be real.

"God damn it! I demand that you breathe! Breathe now, Daddy. Just breathe now for me."

My tears won't stop streaming. Suddenly everything seems to be happening so fast. The blunt weight force of death is taking over him. Great shaking sobs are coming over me. Everything is moving in slow motion and it seem like time is standing still. Slowly he is descending into death. I think he is aware of his own impending circumstance. He looks so uncomfortable and ill at ease. Oxygen is in short supply to his ailing body, as I see the color of his lips begin turning from a natural pink to a sickening deathly shade of blue.

Placing the heel of my nervous left hand on his breastbone, I then place the palm of my right hand over my left as I had learned previously. My arms are tight, rigid and ready to go. God, please help me do this. I need to stop my hands from trembling and get through this. My heart is racing and I can't stop sweating. My dad's eyes are closed but mine are wide open and full of tears. I need him in my life and I'm not sure where I'll turn, or who to, without him. He's touched my life very deeply. My stomach is turning in knots and my shoulders are heavy. I've never witnessed anyone die except in the movies. My dad doesn't have Hollywood symptoms with overly dramatic chest pains, screams and moans. I'm failing my dad with each of my compressions. He's now lost consciousness. Frustration runs rapid and all I want to do is make him live. He's not an actor, but my own flesh and blood, dying right in front of my tearful eyes. All hope is beginning to evacuate the room, which is now closing in on me. Hope is becoming more dark and lifeless with each passing second. The sweat continues to pour down my face. I'm scrambling to help reactivate his unresponsive body. Where's the fucking ambulance?

I continue chest compressions, but his life is coming to an abrupt end. Caught in a rainstorm of sweat, I can no longer behave courageously. Daddy is losing his battle to live and I'm witness to his final moments and I'm not ready. I can't make his heart work any longer. This is absolutely killing me and I can't take it. My heart is heavy as the seconds tick by and disappear within this golden hour, and the paramedics still haven't arrived. Am I having hallucinations? This can't be real. I feel such betrayal as my daddy is being taken away from me.

This isn't fair! There is so much I need to confess to him to make things better between us. I know that life is short but this is way too fast. I've not said everything that I want to say to him. I've wronged and I need to express my deep feelings to him. Time stands still. My dad's heart is losing the battle, giving up and is surrendering. There is no more time to burn and his strength is gone.

Tears pour down my face as I look down at his lifeless body.

"No! Don't do this to me! I'm your little girl! Do you hear me? I want one more breath from you Dad. I know you can do it! Please breathe for me. Please Dad! Dad?"

I've no sense of place or time, just an endless last moment with my dad.

I feel an utter sense of relief as I hear the approaching sirens and see flashing lights as the paramedics arrive and rush in through the open front door to assist. The room quickly fills with lots of people in uniform. Each face is a blur. It feels so wrong. So many questions, and all I can think of at this moment is to pray for my dad.

Lots of questions, like "When did he stop breathing?" "Can you hear me?" "Does he have any allergies?" "What medications is he on?" "Breathe, Francis!" All the while oxygen, defibrillation, medication and chest compressions are taking place. What they are doing isn't working.

"Can you sign a consent form?"

The room is echoing with constant motion around me. It's my dad's fucking video game with monitors, lights and sounds all whirling around me.

I can't keep my control in this insane madness. It's like an out-of-body experience and I'm witnessing it all from above. I just want to walk away because I'm not strong enough to do this.

"Please wake up Dad."

He's dying right in front of my eyes. I know he would want his last rites said. So, in my hour of need I pray as hard as I can.

"Dad, have mercy on me for I have sinned. Lord, I'm not worthy to receive you but only say the word and I shall be healed. God, in your great kindness. Glory be to the Father, Son and Holy Spirit."

I can't stop crying.

"My father entered my home, and may he be surrounded by angels. He serves you O Lord, you are holy, you are kind, abide with the Holy Spirit forever and ever. May almighty God have mercy on you. Forgive you of your sins and lead you to everlasting life. Amen."

The paramedics lift my father's lifeless body onto a gurney, out of the house and into the back of their ambulance, and rush him to the local hospital. I drive tearfully behind in my car, following the flashing red and white lights, and praying for a miracle.

Upon arrival at the hospital his body is taken into the building, and I'm ushered into an empty waiting room filled with rows of black plastic chairs, where I'm asked to sit and wait for news.

After what seems like the longest time the door opens and I'm approached by a doctor with a somber look on his face who says, "I'm so sorry my dear, but your father has gone."

"Can I see him?" I ask.

"Yes, of course you can. Please follow me," he gently responds, and I'm led into the hospital mortuary viewing room.

I see that the familiar color of life has drained from my father's lifeless body and the look on his face is one of peace. I know that my father has accepted the Father and is finally with him and in his loving arms. Consciousness is no longer present or evident. The cogito Descartes famously quoted no longer applies for my father. Death has succeeded. No more pain, no more to suffer. I motion the sign of the cross over my father's body. His life has now reached its end. Mine continues. I'm left alone to figure it out.

When Dad died, a part of me died too. I've never been close to my brother, but now is the time to contact him. It seems like I've forgotten how to dial the phone. My damn fingers won't work. Shaking and trembling I try hard to recall the number I've dialed a thousand times. I have to search my directory to help my confused mind and weak heart. A deep conversation is on the menu for today. I can barely get out a "Hello."

Adam answers the phone in his usual cheerful, upbeat tone. Even at 9:42 p.m. he sounds like he's full of energy.

"He's gone, Adam. Dad is gone."

I can't contain my uncontrollable sobs.

"Gone where? What do you mean, Sammie? What's happened?"

Adam asks basic questions that I struggle to answer. I start thinking about the way he died, and my replies lack clarity and coherence. Adam keeps asking the same questions over and over, until I'm able to clearly explain in tearful detail the evenings events.

"Oh no. I'm so sorry and saddened to hear this. You are so brave for being there and with him in his final moments."

Funny, until he mentioned it, I didn't think I was brave. It was like an out-of-body experience and I didn't even consider giving myself any credit for being there and witnessing his passing. It was forced upon me. I had no choice. I acted out of necessity and duty, and did everything that I possibly could.

"Hey Sis, I know there is a lot of distance between us. Not just physically across the whole country, but we are different spirits."

His voice remains calm and echoes with boldness.

I want to crawl up in a ball. Hide from all that I'm feeling. I'm not used to confrontation or even examining myself for that matter. It's hard to look into the mirror of self-realization. Silence ensues. What can I say to that? My numbness isn't bigger than myself. Adam's light starts to shine through.

"You know Sis. I know this is a difficult time for all of us, but you were the one that was there for Dad in the end. What a great gift you were given, on a spiritual level. You were his strength to see him to the end of his life. May he rest in peace knowing that a loved one was there to the bitter end when he closed his eyes and took his final breath on this earth. Sammie, His light is shining down on you now. It's your job to continue learning the lessons of life."

I'm stunned and shocked. My brother and I have never had a heart to heart like this, and Dad's death is the unfortunate event that's bringing us together. We're able to carry on a conversation without bitterness, eye rolling or jealousy. In the past, it was almost like we had an allergy to each other. We avoided situations in order to not suffer the exaggerated responses that came with the territory. Overwhelming feelings of family rush over me. I need it at this very moment, and the time to understand myself.

"Sammie, you will have a lot of time to contemplate his passing. Life is for the living. Also, look at your own self in the process and the gifts that you have. Don't be afraid. I don't know if I'm wasting my breath, but God will always be with you and love you no matter what. Try to love yourself."

My brother's honest and heroic words do indeed make an impression. He agrees to fly out as soon as he can to help with funeral arrangements.

"Someone needs to tell mom. I've too many walls with her and I know she'll act even crazier and go off the deep end with anger and resentment when she hears the news."

"I think it's best to leave that conversation for the professionals to handle."

After he hangs up the phone, I'm left thinking about all that he's just said.

Slowly in this process, I have to learn to confront all the things that I've been avoiding. I continue to have self-doubt and "if only" questions running through my head, and eventually fall asleep.

For the longest time, I sit in the room where Dad died, replaying last night's senselessly tragic event, over and over. I relive it all again in slow motion, analyzing every detail as it happened, trying to work out whether the outcome could have been changed had I responded differently. My mind tortures itself with infinite improbable probabilities and possibilities.

I've touched upon four of Kübler-Ross' Five Stages of Grief in the hours that have since passed, experiencing denial, anger, bargaining, and depression. My emotions are on high alert and are all over the place. Acceptance is one emotion I know I'll have to shelve for later. This last one is going to be the hardest one for me to reconcile. I'm just not ready to come to terms with my loss yet, and I have a lot left to learn in this world. Perhaps, when I can make peace with myself and fully understand this situation I'll begin to find acceptance, however long that may take. I find it hard to offer myself comfort while my mind is racing. I can't easily accept Dad's death like I'm ordering something from a restaurant menu. It's so much more complex a process. How long will I need to grieve, and should I put a time limit on my grief? Will time heal all my wounds and make me a person better able to accept the things that I can't change? Will another door open now that this one has closed? Grief is a personal feeling, and loss a personal experience, but I'm yet to validate my own feelings. That's something I didn't go to school or prepare for, like taking an exam. Is it good that my dad has died? Is he at peace and no longer in pain or suffering? Should I be angry with God for taking him away from me? Is he now in Heaven and happy to be with God? So many questions run around my head, all unanswered. Why can't I find solace in quotes such as "everything happens for a reason" or "it is God's will?" I'm not perfect and neither is my thinking process. I ask God to guide me in my thoughts and make me stronger during my prayers. One thing I do know is that Dad loved me, and he knew that I loved him too. Both of us can rest in peace with that, until we are together again. I've sinned and I'm a broken person, but I'm certain that God will continue to love and accept me for who I am.

There's a knock at the door, although I'm not expecting anyone. I've no idea what time it is, or the last time I've eaten. I hear a familiar voice that I haven't heard in a very long time.

"Hello, it's me!"

It's like taking a trip down memory lane hearing Mary Whitaker's voice. She's a regular at my local church, and is standing there at my front door, wearing the same old navy pea coat that she's always styled. She's like an angel who's come to my rescue and save me from my thoughts. It's funny how things happen when you least expect it. Does everything really happen for a reason? Is this one of those instances? People come and go without an expected purpose, perhaps only to bring comfort and guidance to a life without direction. "We come to interrupt this program for an important message has just played out in real life." My thoughts are distracted by this great breath of light into my life. My heart is open and ready to accept all that's offered to me.

"Hello, my dear child."

She wraps her arms around me and gives me the biggest darn hug that seems to last for an eternity.

"I'm so sorry to hear the news about your dad. I've known your family for years. Francis was a great man who will be sadly missed by the community and church."

She looks directly into my eyes and I know that she's sincere with her words and gestures.

It suddenly occurs to me that we are still standing in the doorway, so I motion for her to come in from the bitter cold.

"I have to get something from the car. I've taken the liberty of making something for you. Give me a moment."

To my surprise, she brings in home-cooked lasagna and garlic bread, just like I remember eating at church pot luck suppers in my childhood. I could never underestimate the power of a nice home-cooked meal when I felt physically and mentally drained. I'd not realized how hungry I am, and eagerly devour the meal that has been made with her loving hands and kind spirit. Her simple act of human kindness really touches my heart and nourishes my soul. I fill her in on the details of Dad's death, and how I've been coping with it since. She listens to every last word and validates all that I'm feeling.

"Honey, your father is now enjoying everlasting life with Christ. We are all God's children. Embrace the gift that He has given you. Your father has the Grace of God so try to be at peace with that."

I find her voice and words soothing, but hard to swallow and take to heart. I'm still feeling fuzzy from all that's happened.

"It all seems to have happened too quickly, and I'm not ready to say goodbye. Even if we didn't always see eye to eye on things I knew I'd always have his voice and advice to listen to. Now that's no longer an option for me. What I wouldn't give to take back some of the things I've said and done."

"Samantha, you can't punish yourself for the relationship that you'd wished you'd had. Know that your father loved you and that he'll continue to live on in your heart."

She gives me a great big reassuring hug.

"You'll always have your daddy's wisdom following you wherever you go."

"Thank you for all that you've done. It is very kind and thoughtful of you," I graciously respond.

"Anytime Samantha. I'm here for you and your family," she says with a loving look.

I nod, deeply impressed by her intense words. We say our goodbyes and I'm once again left alone with my own thoughts, contemplating all that I've been through recently. I pray to the Father, for my father, and for the strength to gain a better understanding and acceptance. Guilt invades my heart and head that I've not reached out to Mom. I know that it's an issue for another day that I'll have to face eventually. The death of my dad is a commanding emotion to deal with, but facing Joshua and Jessica and telling them of their Grandfather's passing, is an event which is intensely powerful and heartbreaking. They have many questions, tears, and despair in their hearts.

Comfort, compassion and dignity is my mission, in order to teach my kids how to deal with their personal loss. I'm their role model from whom they are to learn about life and death. I know that I've recently abandoned them by my own pursuits of self-discovery. All that I deal with is overwhelming at times, but maintaining grace to develop healthy relationships is my new goal. Their hearts mean everything to me right now, and I'm not going to break them anymore.

A couple of days later we go through the motions at the funeral home for the visitation. The silence in the car is unbearable. It commands its presence like an imposing church service where the congregation falls silent in prayer. The atmosphere feels distinctly oppressive and awkward.

I take a deep breath.

"Come on kids, we must go to the funeral home to say one last goodbye to Granddad."

In essence, it isn't about me anymore. Hope is lost in their eyes as it searches for its new home. This is something bigger. Allowing my kids to witness raw grief and the finality of death.

Tears fill their blue eyes as they gaze at the open casket, and silence fills them as they stare at their Grandfather who looks much changed since they last saw him. Jess, the strong one, stares blankly, trying to make sense of it all. Fear grips my heart as I wonder if I'm strong enough to hold it together, and not wail in emotional pain. I need to be strong for the kids' sake. We stand over his lifeless body together, and I grab my kids' hands firmly and start reciting the Lord's Prayer.

Our Father who art in heaven, hallowed be thy name. Thy kingdom come, thy will be done, on earth, as it is in heaven. Give us this day our daily bread, and forgive us our trespasses, as we forgive those who trespass against us. And lead us not into temptation, but deliver us from evil.

We all say Amen and look solemnly at his body and then at each other. Tears trickle down my face as they join the ones marching down their cheeks. We hug one another like we've never hugged before.

The following day the funeral is held at St. Mary's Catholic Church in Newport. Inside the church I meet my brother, old friends, relatives and new people that were in my parent's lives that I've heard of, but never before met. Mom is there, but she looks heavily drugged and numb. At some level, I feel comforted that she's too loaded to realize the intensity of the day's events. She's a robot without feeling and it's too hard for me to reach out to her.

The magnificent stained glass is there to view as I sing hymns and reflect on my dad's great life. The saints and depictions of Jesus' life contained within the colorful glass add comfort. My sobs are under control until the choir sings my favorite hymn, "Song of the Body of Christ." I've come to share my story with Him and all the purity of it. It provides hope and helps heal my broken soul. Tears fill my eyes as the words cut through to my heart. The song resonates with me. I'm ready to accept all that has happened. This is the breath of life that I need to continue to make a change in my life.

~ Recipe 9 ~
Trying To Move Forward

Prep time: Six days
Serves: Two

This recipe will bring out the best in me. Learning to accept the ingredients that are around me, will bring a deeper meaning. Once my feet are wet, I will be able to see all the obstacles in my way. It will be a bright sunshiny day once the pain has gone. Negative feelings will disappear.

Creativity: Write an apology letter
Cost: Raise money for charity
Culinary: Eat Spanish food
Culture: Ride a boat
Connect: Fight for a cause

The crowds that surrounded my family have left, and the room is quiet again. My brother and I managed to bond and reminisce about our memories of Dad. I wish that heaven had visiting hours where I could bear my soul to my dad and confess all that I've learned about myself in the process. I'm once again faced with silence in my three-bedroom home. I'm now comfortable with who I am and how I express myself.

My dad was the first person to teach me about love. Sometimes, we were both incredibly stubborn, both full of determination. I've learned a lot about myself in the last few months. I've learned how to explore and discover my sexuality. I've challenged my limits and identified my vulnerabilities. I understand how to trust and have faith in myself. I look in the mirror and realize that I am a beautiful person, inside and out. With my philosophical pen at hand I decide to write one last intimate letter to my dad.

Dear Dad,

I can't imagine life without you on this earth. It's hard to write this apology letter, but I must for my own conscience and growth. Each day that passes, I am blessed that I had many wonderful moments with you that will always stay with me. You will never completely understand what I've learned from you. A special place in my heart exists for you. Your smile of approval was all that I ever wanted. I remember the time that you sang songs to me in the car, like Elvis singing "I want you, I need you, I love you," during our trips to southern Texas on Interstate 35. Daddy, I will always remember those cherished words and l will love you with all my heart for the rest of my days. I may have become busy with day-to-day activities and things you disapproved of in my life. I know that I didn't always listen to your sound advice but I heard your words. It made an impact on who I am today. Sometimes children do not always hear the first message of wisdom from their parents until they fall, or discover life for themselves. I must be completely honest with you, my God and myself. I know that I have sinned, but I have faith in forgiveness and resurrection. In this world, I constantly challenge myself to do better. I would like you to think of me as a confident, strong woman who has learned life's lessons well. Sometimes I struggle, but respect that I'm finding myself. I would call myself tenacious in my ability to never give up on the demands and challenges of life. I learned my ability to fight the fight from you. Perhaps, I did not master them all, but I gave every attempt at doing so with my head held high and with no regrets. You taught me how to tie my shoelaces, how to be polite, how to ride a bike, to learn to stop to appreciate those around me and be grateful. We laughed hard at the foolish mistakes I made, and you managed to turn it into another of life's lessons. You covered all that a dad should to help his daughter grow into a fine young lady. Wherever I turned, I knew that you were in the end the one I wanted to turn to. You were my personal police officer and gate-keeper who would protect me from harm. I cannot make excuses for all that I've done or did not do in your big old teddy bear eyes. For that, I'm deeply sorry. It pains me that I was not able to express my love to you on an ongoing basis. I will always know that you will be here with me although you physically aren't. Not a day will go by that I will not have loving thoughts of you until my last breath. But I'm comforted to know that I've learned a great deal from you. Daddy, you will always be my hero and I know that in the end you were looking out for me. Maybe it took a tragedy like this to make me stop in my tracks and recognize all that I have left to live for in this world. I continue to learn, grow and strive to be the person you want me to be. I'm not perfect and temptation is always at my back. God has wiped away my tears and continues to strengthen me. I owe you so much for the many gifts you have given me. The most important gift you gave me was love. Please continue to guide me all the rest of my days and whenever the wind is at my back.

Always,
Your Little Girl

Five days later, I feel that there's a lot that I want to accomplish in my father's name. Without a job to tie me down, I feel the need to find a purpose to connect and motivate me. While breezing through the Newport Daily News, I come across an advertisement for the American Heart Association. Cardiovascular disease and stroke are the leading causes of death in southern New England. My dad was one of the unfortunate victims of this illness. Rereading the powerful message of the cause I can't escape its meaning. I decide that I will donate money and raise awareness on "National Wear Red Day." It also happens to coincide with what would have been my father's birthday. I've always thought of red as being a color full of confidence and allure. If a woman wears red, that changes everything, I think. Her attitude is uplifted and she is ready to take on the world. I put on a newly purchased cocktail dress.

Today is a bitterly cold day. The wind greets me, and leaves its presence on my exposed cheeks with a touch of red. Inside, I continue to have the warmth of my dad touching my heart. I know he's with me, looking down on me from heaven and smiling. Sometimes things feel more intense than I'm able to express in words. I head to the brunch meeting where there are many people who have similar stories and passions in their hearts to help others. The room is filled in solidarity with red-inspired fashions. Together we help raise money and awareness, which is an important part of my journey. I want to make a real positive difference in the lives of others.

I put my social skills to the test by deciding to join the fund-raising group I've just met at the local eatery. The song "Lady In Red" by Chris De Burgh echoes in my head as I think about how men sometimes can't remember what a woman was wearing the first time they met, although I guess there will be no problem doing so at a "red" event. As I walk out of the ladies room trying to fix the purse strap that has caught on my right shoulder, my eye catches a distinguished looking man. He is wearing a New York Yankees baseball hat, a sports jacket, short straight blonde hair and facial stubble. He's wearing the biggest grin in the joint. Normally, I would let my gaze meet the floor, but our eyes connect the moment that I walk in his direction. He stands up, probably in mid-sentence to the guy on his left. I confidently smile back at him and start walking towards him. No way am I going to let this opportunity pass me by. My conviction is spilling over and in his direction.

"That suits you," he says, nodding at me in approval.

"Why, thank you."

I smile and stop to gaze at him more closely. He's picture perfect in every detail.

"My name is Stephen Walker. It's a pleasure to meet you!"

His eyes are intense blue with a hint of warm golden flecks. I pick up from his accent that he's definitely a city boy from the Northeast. For some reason, I notice his gold-toned square sports watch as he extends his hand to give mine a firm handshake. Surely, this is fate and my dad's approval is looking down on me. I can't have been luckier than to meet such a handsome man to boost my confidence. He seems equally engaged and interested in my charms.

"Hello Stephen. I'm Samantha, but my friends call me Sammie."

I tilt my head and coyly smile at him in a flirtatious manner.

This man is stunning and natural with a classic Americana look. He's wearing a pair of blue jeans, which look like they were made for his body. He melts me with his powerful rugged shoulders. For a brief moment we look directly into each other's eyes. He takes my breath away as I stand there in his presence. An overwhelming feeling comes over me, unlike one that I've felt before.

"Actually, Sammie I would be really pleased if I could get to know you a little better. May I buy you a drink?"

"Sure," I reply and we head to the bar.

He comes across as real and genuine with a pure soul. The room is closing in and it feels like it contains only him and me. There is no pressure as our words start to flow effortlessly. Curiosity about everything erupts as I gaze at him.

"What brings you to these neck of the woods?" I ask softly.

"Whatcha mean? I can't fool you that I'm a native to these parts?" he grins.

Our laughter is in sync like we are two people mimicking each other.

"Whatcha mean?"

I flirtatiously mimic his mannerisms. I grab his Yankees hat and put it on my head.

"Does it look better on this native head than a foreigner?"

I can't believe I'm so bold and testing the territory.

"Yes, Sammie, that does suit you," he says, surprised by my temerity.

His eyes twinkle and he moves closer. I pause for a moment taking it all in. His beauty and charm seem too good to be true.

"So, ask me any question and I'll try to answer it."

"That's an invitation I can't resist. How about, who is the most important person in your life?"

Like a falling star, I think of my father. He intently zeros in on my response.

"Stephen, my dad recently passed away. I don't think he realized it, but he was the most important person in my life. I think sometimes I took him for granted and didn't always show him what he meant to me, but deep down I know that he always wanted what was best for me."

Too bad it's taken a tragedy for me to get these words out. My walls are down and I'm feeling vulnerable to his next response.

He turns to me like an old friend and gives me a hug without hesitation.

"Sammie, I'm so sorry to hear your news."

He gazes at me. I stop and without hesitation realize that he has empathy and good looks all rolled into one.

I stand there in reverence of his gentleness.

"You are an old soul. Thank you for that."

We continue talking about my dad and his meaning in my life. Stephen is relaxed and interested. He appears to be comfortable with our conversation as if it's second nature. The more I reveal, the more I see his warmth and charming personality. He listens, enraptured with a captivated ear.

In turn, I ask questions about how he ended up in this part of the world. He recounts that he's on assignment working on a contract with another local business. His main headquarters are in New York City. He's hard working and supports the most successful baseball club in history, unless a Red Sox fan has something to say otherwise. I continue to quiz him on his interests in sports and express to him my passion of music. I'm equally thrilled by how much we have in common, as we continue talking effortlessly. As the clock strikes two, Stephen turns to me.

"Meet me at Bowen's Wharf at around 3:45 p.m." he says, smiling with his deep commanding voice. "I will have a surprise waiting for you."

He grins like a boy with a great big treat on Christmas Day.

"You are too charming! I will need to run home and get a change of clothes."

I glance at him. I've no idea what he has in mind.

"Sammie, don't take too long. I'll see you in less than two hours, OK?" he says softly. "Oh, and here is my cell number in case anything happens unexpectedly and you need to call me."

"I will do exactly as you ask," I say with an excited smile. I give him a slight hug and make my departure.

I arrive at home shortly afterward. It's quite a rush as I run around trying to find the perfect outfit to accompany my new man. I must think practical and warm for my mystery rendezvous. There is a knock at the door. I'm not quite ready for unsolicited visitors, as I wander around the house in my pink robe and red lace panties. I'm almost ready to go. I don't have time for this right now.

Knock. Knock. It's getting louder.

"For Heaven's sake, I'm coming! Hang on a minute!" I mutter under my breath.

I get to the door, then, without even glancing I hurriedly open it and find him standing there. I can't even begin to react, seeing my ex-husband unexpectedly standing in front of me. My heart starts to pound as flashbacks from my past start to haunt me. Inside, I'm in turmoil and it hits me like a tornado. I want to hide and retreat into my world. There is a moment's silence, which seems like the longest time as we stand and stare at each other.

"Samantha, you look great! Your hair looks so different. You've had it all chopped off!" he says while staring at me. I'm not sure what to do or say, as I stand here, frozen to the spot.

"I wanted to say that I'm sorry to hear about your father, and that I didn't make it to his funeral. He was a good man," he exclaims, while stepping towards me through the doorway, and putting his uninvited hand on my shoulder. I squirm and can't even look him directly in the eye. My breathing is getting rapid. I'm getting vulnerable as he moves towards me.

"Samantha, I've been thinking about you a lot lately," he says gently, and moves his hand through my hair. I must be strong. I can handle this.

"No!"

I shake my head.

"Your timing is bad. I was just about to go out."

I glance up at him.

"I've always loved you," he continues.

He's playing with my head. He thinks that he can just turn up, strut his stuff and have me at his mercy. I'm stronger than that. I'm no longer the woman he once had.

"I'm a different person now. I've moved on," I manage to mutter.

He stares at me in disbelief because I've challenged his words.

"I don't know what to say," he replies, shaking his head.

"I'm no longer your doormat. I deserve so much more than you ever appreciated me for."

Momentum and power fills my voice.

"This is a side of you that I haven't seen before," he says.

"I want you to think long and hard about us, Samantha, because I know that we still have something. We have a history together. You can't escape the past."

"No, that something left a long time ago when you took me for granted and hurt me. I can remember all the negative history we had."

I stand firm on my words. He leans over despite what I've just said to him, and plants a kiss on my gentle lips. He presses hard against me like he's never kissed me before. His lips are persistent and eager. He tantalizes me with his power and the taste of his desires.

Pushing hard against me, I find it difficult to resist someone who wants me so deeply and that I've known inside and out. His display of passion is evident as he grabs me tightly, brushing against my breasts with his firm chest. Closing my eyes, I'm helpless to his controlling nature. Knowing how turned on he is, as his breath is heavy, I'm getting pulled into his ways and am at his mercy.

He kisses me deeply and throws his tongue into my mouth. I can taste his salty tongue and smell his familiar scented cologne. It does feel good to be wanted, but I know deep inside that this is wrong on so many levels.

"No," I murmur with incredulity that he wants me like he's never wanted me before.

"I want you right now, God damn it! We need this. I need this."

With that he pushes the door shut, and unzips his brown pants which drop to the floor. He slips my robe from my shoulders, and it slides to the floor. With easy access to my panties, he pulls them down and plants his hard cock right against me.

I'm caught up in the moment, as he pushes me against the wall. Taking a deep breath he plunges his cock deep inside me. It's unexpectedly rough and firm. He admonishes me.

"That will teach you to stay away from me. I've got more for you," he breathes.

He slides his cock in and out, grabbing my buttocks firmly with his hands and pushing his cock deeper inside me. I can't help but moan as I'm taken off guard. He moves, twists and turns his cock so hard. I try hard to not let go but it's so difficult to resist.

I groan. He looks down at my breasts and notices my Fleur-de-lis.

"Mmm, Baby got a new tattoo. You are a naughty, naughty girl!"

He starts licking hard at my erect pink nipples that have become magnetized by his dominance. Anxiety, fear, thrill and excitement are all spinning around my head. His turn on is evident as he fucks me like an animal with his horny passion.

"I want you so bad, and I'm going to give you all that I've got."

He thrusts his cock deeper and deeper inside me. He squeezes me tightly and his movements are fast and rough.

Holy Shit! I can't believe this is happening. I inhale and try to move but he won't let go of me. He kisses my neck and has found my pleasure points. I close my eyes and am in shock at my own helplessness. This is so fucking wrong!

"Please!"

I can't control his actions. He continues and won't stop. His energy is like a wrestler who is going for the state championship and I'm his prize. I'm his doormat once again, as he takes me in this passive upright position.

Fear grips me. I don't know how to respond. This is the man that I had spent the majority of my life with, day in and day out. Years went by without even a warm caress or sensual love-making session, and now he's fucking me like I'm some porno star. I don't know what to make of it. He groans, with quick shallow breaths, as his sweat slides against my pale white skin. He gives me more and more kisses with all his power and might. He's taking me prisoner and I can't stop him.

He's beyond aroused and ready to conquer me over and over. He doesn't stop, and unleashes his tongue all over my body. I grab his hair and take a deep breath. Ooh, he keeps pounding me real good. I'm embarrassed that I can't stop the sensations that I'm feeling. He has hit my G-spot. My body responds without my mind's permission. I feel guilty at the pleasure that's happening between my legs. Ahh, it has been so long since he's ever given me pleasure. I'd forgotten what it felt like with this man.

I don't have the strength to combat him but I beg, "You have to stop!"

"I will stop when I'm good and ready and you are going to like it. Every last ounce that I give you."

He commands me and stares me down. I don't know where this is coming from. He's going to make me cum whether I like it or not.

He pushes harder and harder and is relentless in his actions. There's no stopping him now. I'm beyond the point of no return. I have to give in because I'm too weak to stop. He's taken no prisoners in his mission to seduce me. Holy Fuck! What have I done? I'm not sure I can handle this.

"Ooh, ooh. No. Don't!"

He thrusts himself and keeps moving, over and over. He has a pounding rhythm inside my body and I quiver and shake. It won't be long before he lets himself go. I close my eyes and let it all release inside. My juices flow in this unexpected forceful passion. My legs tense and move with his movements.

He groans some more and lets out a big deep orgasm, shooting his hot load deep inside me. He shakes and moves intently.

"Oh Samantha, you feel so goddamn hot!"

He melts deep into me. I'm breathless. This is not the man that I was married to for all those years. This is someone else that I've not seen. I don't even think I know this man. I feel like a stranger has just seduced me. I don't know what to make of it or how to respond. Maybe it's part of his plan, but it isn't what I had in mind. He always has a way of playing with my head and this has definitely topped the list. Hands down, he's succeeded in fucking with my head once again, but I can't let it show how fucking vulnerable I am right now. I don't know why I keep making these mistakes when it comes to men. Especially my ex! This wasn't supposed to happen. It's not the love that I wanted or the way that I wanted it, but at least I know that I'm irresistible to this man. For once in my life he really wanted me, something I rarely felt in our marriage. Maybe that's why I succumbed to his desires. I am filled with cracks and flaws and desperately try to stay focused.

Speechless, I grab the door handle to gain my balance.

He looks straight at me and says, "I needed that. It was damn good!"

He looks slowly over his conquest.

I take a deep breath. Why did I let myself succumb to him? Have I not learned anything from my long, lifeless, loveless marriage? This unexpected turn of events has me confused.

He kisses me again and slightly caresses my arm.

"Right, we need to do this again sometime. But next time I will see to it that you are more comfortable and giving the fucking pleasures right back to me."

His lips curl with an "I won" smile. I flush and he winks at me, gathers himself and rushes out the door. I look down and note that my sexual encounter is at the cost of my guilt.

Having realized that I've been taken off guard, I need to pick myself up again. This unexpected sexual rendezvous is something I never imagined would happen. What a complete and utter fool I am. Shit! I look at the time and realize that I'd forgotten all about meeting up with Stephen and the arrangement that we had made earlier. An overwhelming sense of shame comes over me, that I let my ex take control of me. How can my ex get away with making me feel so bad? His past putdowns made me weak, but now his dominance over me has made me submissive. He's probably laughing at me right now and thinks that he can get what he wants when he wants.

I must not get worried about that now. It's not important to my new start. I have to move away from my past. I can't be a prisoner to his ways. Reminding myself what he's done, and the pain he's caused, is all the medicine I need to take right now to clear my emotions, re-establish myself and take back control of my life.

Time to move onto a new man and scent in my life. I need to have hope that there is something better for me in this world. My heart is vulnerable and hasn't been protected. Where are my friends when I need them to ask for advice?

I could quickly phone up Maria or Guy. They understand me. They won't lecture me about how I succumbed to my ex. They'll support me without giving me the riot act about my actions.

Shit! No time to waste. I jump in the shower for a quick rinse to wash away my impurity. I quickly put on my navy pants, black boots and striped top for my casual encounter. Hurriedly, I brush my just-fucked hairdo. I fling my things into my little silver Toyota Corolla and drive faster than the speed of light, within Newport's speed limits, of course. Life is complicated enough without getting a damn speeding ticket too. I can't deal with too many distractions. I need to stay focused for the next turn of events and be ready. For what, I'm not quite sure.

Arriving at the dock fifteen minutes late, in the hope of finding Stephen, I notice that it's unusually mild for this time of year. The seaside village atmosphere of Narragansett Bay has familiarity and welcomes me, evoking childhood memories. I pull up in the market square, and after paying for metered parking head towards the water. There he stands, outside Bowen's Ferry Landing, waiting for me with his mouth slightly open with an, "I'm your dream date here to rescue you" smile.

Holy shit, he looks so fucking irresistible. He walks towards me, and greets me with a big hug and a kiss on the cheek. His deep sapphire blue eyes burn right through me. I'm like a deer caught in his headlights, my heart pounding with fear and thrilling excitement. Thirty minutes ago I had some fucking wild sex forced upon me by my ex-husband and I'm afraid he will notice the scent. But I'm also thinking how lucky I am to be with such a handsome mysterious man. I keep repeating to myself, how did I get so lucky? Could he be the one? I can feel my heart beating strongly, the blood pumping through my veins, and my cheeks flush.

"Sammie, I wasn't sure whether you were going to turn up. I was beginning to think that you'd chickened out on me, or were playing hard to get."

He raises an outstretched arm and takes my hand. He wastes no time in getting into my personal space.

I grin, "I wanted to make sure that I made the right impression for you and get it just right."

"You certainly have, from what I've seen so far. I'm well pleased with what you have to offer," he says appraising my appearance.

"I want you to trust me, Sammie. My intentions are purely honorable."

I gaze at him and smile back. I've had so many trust issues in the past. Men have let me down so many times. I need to have faith in Him that He will deliver. It's hard for me to let go and believe that this could be true. I need to trust in my instincts and Him that this will not be another fruitless search for love.

"I feel so comfortable around you Sammie," he says, glancing at me.

"I like that about you. You speak so warmly," I reply. My eyes dance with his. There is definitely an unquestionable chemistry.

"It's like I don't have to pretend around you. When I look at you I feel something wild."

His eyes are all over me.

"Maybe I feel like you get what I'm feeling too," he continues.

I gaze at him studiously. I'm not sure if I'm a fool believing in instant attraction, but I've a gut feeling about this man. I need to take a risk and let it out on the line. Being honest with my feelings, I hope that he's genuine in his intent with every step we take.

We head to the waterfront and he leads me aboard an educational vessel. He clearly knows the three other crewmembers on board, which has me deeply intrigued. Showing excitement and curiosity for this new adventure, I'm open and willing to accept what he has to offer. He doesn't let me out of his sight. I can feel him in my every movement, like he's studying me, absorbing every detail.

Right now, we are inseparable, like two high school kids who are connecting and bonding.

On the surface the peaceful waters appear still, with a glass-like appearance, but our boat can feel the almost visually imperceptible motion of the bay. As we set sail, heading away from the shoreline, the ship begins to provide breathtaking views of Newport Harbor.

Stephen tells me that he's a volunteer for an ecological group called the Bay Preservation Society, who's ethos is to protect the local natural habitat, and try to ensure that the coastal waters are kept clean and free of pollution, for the benefit of humans and mammals alike. He tells me that the group aims to protect, restore, and improve the bay, while also informing and educating the public to the importance of maintaining the areas environmental health.

As we sail towards Rose Island, with its pretty lighthouse, he hands me a pair of binoculars while giving me expert narration about the importance of protecting the marine life and the food chain. He tells me that hundreds of seals migrate to the bay each winter, before heading towards the Gulf of Maine in mid-spring. He points to the rocks off the island, and to my amazement I can see many Harbor seals, in great close-up detail, resting above the waterline. I had no idea that seal stay here over the winter. How fascinating!

This intelligent man, who is not only goddamn hot and attractive, but also shows concern for the community and environment, immediately turns me on. He reveals a compassionate side to his personality, filled with selfless motives. I begin to understand how he wants to change the world around him, and make it a better place through his actions. How I admire a man with acts of such decency.

Watching the calm waters and taking in the natural wonders, I begin to feel a deeper connection with myself. This inner peace continues to pervade my soul and bring me back to reality. Realizing that even the smallest actions can make a big difference and help the world around me, begins to unfold a part in my heart. This inner light was missing before. Lost, hidden or buried somewhere along the way. Its rediscovery melts my heart and makes me feel pure joy again, for the first time in a long time. I'm open to expose myself to the work around me in a positive light. The song "This Little Light of Mine" comes into my head, and I sing the lyrics silently in my mind.

I need to let the love shine in my heart and uncover the gifts that it has to offer. I feel sad for the recent loss of my dad, but I'm not afraid to deal with the messy emotions that come with death. My father's death has forever changed my life. I can no longer reach out and phone my dad when something good happens in my life. Dad would be the first person I would call to share information. I hide my tears when I think of him. There is no one that misses him more than me. I need to set the pace of how I deal with death. He was a gift to me and that gift will forever live on in my heart. The fact that I will stumble and fall on my journey to deal with my grief is one I need to accept. It's strange, but even at this moment I'm taken off guard by thoughts that creep in, of dealing with the emotional impact. Maybe my short-tempered ways have surfaced as I deal with confrontation. I find it hard to not hit the "send button" hastily when I'm faced with problems on the fly. Immediate gratification and notification are done instinctively. I didn't expect that I would be hit with these thoughts at this moment and time. It's hard to contain them all. I need to smile at the world, although I've been crying deeply on the inside.

It's funny that when you least expect it these emotions start flooding in. Nothing will ever take these feelings away. They are genuine and heartfelt.

Stephen notices I'm quiet and pondering and asks, "Whatcha thinking sweet one?"

"Oh, just thinking of my father and a song popped into my head. You will think it's silly."

"Give me a try."

"Just inspired that's all. You heard of a Gospel song called "This Little Light of Mine?" The energy behind it. I feel the energy and peacefulness around you. With you I feel the light."

"Why, thank you!" he winks at me.

"I feel at peace. Thanks for bringing me here," I smile.

Stephen lightens the mood with a shuffle dance and playfully exclaims, "Or how about "This Little Girl of Mine" by Ray Charles? Now that's a classic secular blues lyric. I would love it if you would be my girl!"

My heart melts at his suggestion. Laughing, I realize we've just connected on a musical level too. The more I see, the more I know we are similar.

We are like two peas in a pod, two of a kind. I know that he is my "Pea."

Sailing around the Narragansett, I'm reminded of all the reasons why I love the timelessness of this 18th century port city. There is no place like home. The panoramic waterfront views are breathtaking. The kids always enjoyed fishing, biking and going to the beach. Not only is the scenery reinvigorating my interest, but also Stephen and his calm demeanor captivate me. My hopes begin to rise. With the passing of time, I become more enchanted.

"I can't believe a fine guy like you is single."

My curiosity has gotten the better of me. Shit! Maybe I shouldn't start a conversation about past lovers on our first encounter. What was I thinking to start asking about his past? To my surprise he answers me directly.

"I've actually enjoyed being single at some points in my life. I became very successful while I was unattached. I dedicated myself to work and that's what I lived and breathed. It became my identity, my purpose in life, and helped define myself. In some respects I was married to my work. It required a lot of working nights and weekends, and endless traveling. I never had time for anything else. Even my mom complained that holidays and birthdays had to be scheduled around my job. I was never in one place very long, but no one but me can complain about what happened."

"I don't get why you have a connection to the bay?" I curiously question.

"Oh. My mother used to bring me and my sister here on summer vacations. I have fond memories of coming to the beach and swimming in the ocean," he recollects with a beaming smile.

"Wow! That's so cool. You know, we might've met on the beach when we were young."

I chuckle at the thought.

"Yeah! But, it wouldn't have worked out because I would've taken your beauty and genuine charm for granted. Sometimes life happens for a reason."

He moves closer to me.

I gaze at him intently. Our worlds seemed so far apart and now they have collided. His intensity rivets me and I'm in awe. Our paths would have never crossed ten years ago. I was busy being a mommy and he was busy being a slave to his job. He lived a powerful and fast-tracked lifestyle, influential and committed to his work. I lived the life of raising my family and taking care of others. Somehow, we both managed to lose our identities to other forces and responsibilities along the way.

"Were you happy?" I ask with interest.

"Sure, it was brilliant. I could do what I want, when I wanted. There was no one to boss me around and tell me what to do. I could make my own timetable. I wasn't accountable to anyone. My time was my own. Going to the bar and hanging out at clubs as long as I wanted was fine. No checking in if I was late, no added drama either. I could watch what I wanted on TV and play my music really loud."

He smiles wistfully.

"How about you Sammie? Are you happy?"

His eyes return my gaze.

"Sure!" I mimic in sarcasm, because I think about his carefree lifestyle, and how he's accountable to no one.

I wonder where I fit in? He doesn't have to chauffeur kids around, stay up late when one of them has a fever, or remind them to do their homework.

"I'm a single mom, recently divorced. I have two kids, Joshua aged twelve and Jessica aged fourteen, who keep me busy with their extracurricular activities of soccer, dance and piano. I spend my life taking care of their needs and running from activity to activity to fulfill them. Oh, and until recently, I worked part-time in an oh so glamorous hair salon."

He picks up on the sarcasm in my voice and tries to lighten the mood.

"Look at you now! My stunning Babe!"

He gently caresses me and moves his hands up and down my arm.

Bashfully I smile.

"It's taken a lot to get me here. Some things I'm proud of and others, not so much, but all were a part of my discovering myself."

Stephen nods.

"I can see that you've spread your wings from the woman that you described before."

I look at Stephen with more insecurity and wonder what we are doing together. He reads my facial expressions so easily.

"Come here my sweet one. I'm not here to make any guarantees that we'll live happily ever after, but from what I've seen and experienced with you today, I know that I don't want to be single anymore. I want someone special with whom to share my excitement and passion. When I make a difference in helping the environment and ecological health of this area, I want to be able to boast to someone about it."

His voice is bold and strong as he speaks with authority.

"I love the enthusiasm that you bring. It's so refreshing."

I hug him and hold him close.

The sun bids goodnight and begins its descent from the sky, casting a warm golden glow over us, as it slowly disappears beyond the horizon.

As we begin our journey south back to the marina, Newport Bridge begins to silhouette itself against the warm-colored reds and oranges that now illuminate the evening sky. The water's surface dances with the lights reflection, as the sun makes its final exit.

This peaceful and colorful display relaxes me and makes me realize what's important.

I take a moment to be thankful that I'm its willing and fortunate audience.

A slight breeze from the east tickles us, as the skies darken and the moonlight becomes more apparent. The waters color changes, now reflecting the moon's silvery light.

Sitting beside each other, holding hands, we take a deep breath together, almost in unison. I'm so grateful that we've found each other.

"All this fresh air has given me an appetite. May I buy you dinner?" he inquires.

"Sure, that would be great!" I warmly respond.

Leaving the marina, my car follows his to the restaurant of his choice. I sense that he's familiar with the territory and I eagerly await his next move. To my surprise, we arrive at a small family-run Spanish restaurant in Narragansett. He orders red sangria and the Paella Valenciana served for two. The dish of shrimp, sea scallops, clams, mussels, chicken, chorizo, calamari, saffron rice and mild spices sings to my taste buds. Seeing Stephen across the table from me, I feel like I'm in an incredible dream, for my journey to this point has been surreal. His eyes meet mine and I'm in a romantic zone, which I don't wish to end.

As our conversation flows, Stephen asks about my family. I realize that I can't escape what exists in my real life, however painful it is for me. This fairytale evening is being challenged. My walls begin to surface and rise with his question. I know that he just wants to get to know me, but am I really ready to lay out and display my deepest emotions to him? My gut instinct tells me to protect myself and ignore his question, or do what I do best and deflect the conversation by answering questions with a question. Maybe I could even alleviate the rising tension I feel with some humor or a joke. How do I deal with my raw emotions? I try deflection.

"Stephen, you know about my dad. What about your family? I don't really know anything about them. Tell me more about your relationship with your sister and your family."

I try to take control of the conversation so I can steer its direction away from my vulnerabilities.

Stephen keeps his smile.

"I couldn't be more proud of my older sister, Eve. She's a veteran of the United States Marines and fought in both the Gulf War and Iraq. She makes me proud to be an American and I salute her bravery. The stories she tells are amazing."

"I would love to meet her one day." I say. "I'm sure I could learn a lot from her."

"Yeah that's something to put on your to-do list for sure." he replies.

He gathers his thoughts and his mind drifts to another place. I see a change in his facial expression, as his eyes take on the sudden appearance of sadness, the corners of his lips begin to droop, and his vocal tone becomes one of solemnity.

"Sammie, my mother died of breast cancer after a two-year battle last spring. It was the most devastating thing for me to have to witness. Cancer sucks! It made me feel numb and so angry at the world for taking her away because she was such an amazing woman."

"Oh Stephen, I'm sorry to hear that. I wish I'd had the chance to meet her. What was her name?"

"Lillian. She was only sixty-seven. Way too young to die. No matter the age, I felt like an orphan afterward. She was my go-to person whenever I needed advice or someone to vent to. She was a strong woman who knew the right words to say to me in times of trouble. My life was turned upside down, and I discovered where I needed to focus my energies. In her honor, I decided to give back to others, and to not just focus on my own endeavors. I returned to the Bay, and each time I join in a cause for the Bay Preservation Society, I get a sense of gratification knowing that her spirit is alive. A continuing sense of connectedness through helping the environment and others," he says proudly.

"I have joy in my heart knowing I can touch and improve the lives of others."

His eyes begin to brighten as he remembers her and his purpose in life.

"I've also met others who are in the same "Cancer sucks club" as me. Losing a loved one to such a terrible disease provides us with commonality and unites us. I've found it very therapeutic meeting people that have gone through similar experiences to me. Finding people who will listen and who can empathize. They have helped me to understand and come to terms with my loss."

"Stephen, you are an amazing man, and I know she would be proud of you, because I sure am."

I smile, touched by his emotional honesty, and reach for his hand.

"Thanks Sammie. I'm glad that we met. I don't mean to monopolize the conversation. How about your mother? Tell me about her. If she's anything like you, I know she will be special."

My heart skips a beat, as I know that there's no avoiding this heart-to-heart. I can't hide under the table or gently excuse myself from this conversation. After he's just poured his heart out to me, it's only fair that I should be square with him, no matter how much he may judge me. I take a deep breath and avert eye contact.

"Umm, she's still alive."

I struggle to mutter the words. It's hard to be bold and say it, to admit that there's a hidden illness that runs in my family that no one is proud of.

All I can murmur out of my mouth, like I'm making a grand confession is, "My mom has bipolar-type schizoaffective disorder."

There! I've finally said those upsetting words out loud and admitted it.

"Oh, I'm so sorry to hear that. I will listen to whatever you want to share."

The floodgates open.

"I've been haunted by it all of my life. When I was young, I never understood why mom had great fits of rage and was angry when I got bad grades, or showed a complete lack of interest in my school choir recitals. She had huge mood swings. Sometimes, ecstatic happiness, at other times catatonic depression. She also tried to commit suicide by overdosing on pills. On other occasions when she wasn't taking her meds, she believed that she was having direct communication with God, and that she was his chosen messenger. I blamed myself for her reckless manic energy that had me walking on eggshells if I did something wrong, like not cleaning my room, or the crazy irrational anger if I came home too late from a friend's house. She would yell and say extremely hurtful things to me and my father. Our house had lots of sleepless nights, punctuated with disagreements and arguments. My brother didn't know how to deal with the problem, so as soon as he was old enough he moved out. I hid for long periods of time because I was scared. I was too young to leave home, so used to spend a lot of time in my mother's closet, dressing up and pretending to be a princess waiting to be whisked away by my prince. Our family was divided. She alienated everyone and even those closest to her. We had to pretend there wasn't a problem and that we were a normal family."

I think about the terrible pain of witnessing Mom going in and out of psychiatric institutions and Dad having to deal with the system. Finding the right balance of doctors and medications could never save her from herself. Flashbacks run rampant through my mind. I'm feeling so vulnerable after all that I've just said.

He blinks, and tries to understand the lifetime of pain, suffering and challenges I've faced. He knows that he's not qualified to fix the problem.

"Sammie, it sounds like you've endured a lot in your life. I'm sorry. I can't imagine how difficult it must be for you and your family to deal with."

Tears run down my face. He's too caring for words and I can't fully comprehend how sweet this man is being to me.

I barely whisper, "Thank you for coming into my life. You appeared right when I needed you the most."

He wipes away my tears and smiles.

"Maybe fate has brought us together. Give me your hand."

He takes it in his, and I hold his tightly.

We each recognize the pain that we've felt in our lives, but move forward in our quest to break down the walls that limit and hold us back. I know that there's something more than what I can see with my eyes.

Who can I turn to in times of trouble? Is it Mother Mary that I should turn to, and will she speak words of wisdom to me, as Paul McCartney suggested in "Let it Be?" How should I cope with problems and situations that I find myself in? Should I run and hide when things get rough? How many more hours of darkness must I endure before I begin to finally see the light? Life is filled with challenges. Maybe being aware of how I handle them is one of the greatest attributes I can acquire. I've been tested many times. Each time I find out more about myself and what really matters. I'm still here, and no matter how many knocks I've taken, I'm still standing. Each day I continue to discover more and more about myself and learn to accept the person that I'm becoming. I know that I'm not perfect and I've never claimed to be. I'm willing to understand and learn from my mistakes so that I can continue to grow. I feel a need to pray and get closer to God to find answers to all of my questions. He will guide me to be a stronger person. The beauty that has touched my soul and my heart is a reminder to me of what life is all about. The joy that I'm feeling in his presence, gives me a sense of possibility and promise. Sometimes in life I can never fully explain why things happen, whether it's by chance, luck, God's will, persistence or fate. Right now, I'm thankful for this experience.

~ Recipe 10 ~
Finding A New Purpose

Prep time: Two days
Serves: Three

During my journey of discovery, I will try different ingredients. Be strong as I share what has influenced me over the years and share them with others. Don't be ashamed of the journey and its process. Finding purpose and meaning in this recipe will provide for a notable ending. Inspire and influence others with this new recipe.

Creativity: Draw in the sand
Cost: Join a class
Culinary: Change diet
Culture: Walk on the beach
Connect: Write a book

We look at each other, not wanting the night to end. He has one last surprise before Cinderella needs to head for home. We drive to Scarborough State Beach. I've been a Rhody for a big part of my life but I never really ventured to these parts. Funny how you can live in an area, but be so busy that you never take time to visit. It takes an outsider to bring you to your own surroundings and make you aware of them. Stephen and I have the entire stretch of ocean to ourselves on this winter evening.

"Close your eyes Sammie."

He holds me close. As he asks, I shut my eyes.

"Listen to the sound of the waves. Hear the voice of the ocean and let it take you away."

He hugs me from behind like a soft, comforting blanket. I listen to his deep Northern accent and feel every breath down my neck. An overwhelming feeling of contentment and security rushes over me. I'm safe and accepted within the depths of his heart.

The soft white sand, illuminated by the bright full moon, and calming sound of ocean waves are relaxing, as the scenery is all to ourselves. There is a beautiful lighthouse down the shore. Walking along the beach listening to the waves, Stephen bends over, and with his finger draws "S and S" with a heart around it. A love message in the sand. The signals are loud and clear that he wants me as much as I want him.

Stephen playfully starts climbing around a rocky outcrop and I follow and frolic around. Then he takes my hand and we climb beyond, to the rocky cliffs, and then up a trail to witness the most amazing views!

Stephen turns to me.

"Sammie this has to be one of the most comfortable and greatest nights I've had in a long time."

He draws his hands around my waist. He moves his hand to my chin and lift it up. Stephen confidently and intimately kisses me. Slowly, his lips move over mine. Eagerly I respond back, for I know that at this magical moment I'm falling deeper and deeper for him. I wrap my arms around him. He's firm, but not controlling or threatening. His soft and gentle kiss is unlike one I've ever experienced before. I've had a thousand kisses in my lifetime. But this one, this first kiss, is the one that has vividly woken me up. My heart was asleep and my soul was lifeless before our lips touched.

In this very moment a spark has erupted and my life is forever changed. My knees are weak and my heart pounding a hundred beats per minute. The kiss lingers and touches my heart as he incorporates his hands and moves them softly against my back. He kisses me and guides his lips feather-softly against the edges of mine. He sweeps me off my feet with just one slow passionate kiss. The atmosphere between us is an unspoken love interest that immediately runs full force. There is no stopping the momentum that's between us.

His lips flow and draw me into his enchanting ways. I begin tracing his lips with my tongue and he parts them slowly. Our tongues dance and move together with passion. I explore his lips more with my tongue. Our mouths are pressed hotly together. The electricity between us could make an ice cube melt in a moment. The taste of his soft lips have me wanting more. My eyes are closed as our bodies press firmly against each other. I can feel every detail of his curved lips and the soft dent in his upper lip. Softly, I put my hands around his neck and run my fingers through his blonde hair. With this firm embrace, I can feel his heart beat and his body melt into mine. Quivering and gently moving, I'm turned on beyond belief with such simple and affectionate movements.

This foreplay has me wanting more but I know that this is just the beginning of something real and I'm willing to wait. Our kisses weave in and out, as our lips touch each other passionately. He could kiss me over and over again like the great poets have said until I lose count. For once, I'm not in a rush to explode with passion.

With each intoxicating kiss, I am bestowed a grand rush of euphoric feelings. I could dance on air. Gently, I bite his lower lip while being sensually aggressive. His firm embrace is his green light that he approves of my moves. Stephen's breathing is ragged as he grabs me firmly. I'm content to savor every ounce of detail with his sweet kisses. Our bodies are entwined and molded into one. It is a truthful, honest moment between two connected souls. The backdrop of the world disappears, as I'm his sole focus. I ask nothing more than to be with a man who will love me and treat me the way I deserve and yearn to be treated. We are locked together in intimacy, as our kisses are the key to our desires.

"I love your sweet kisses," I whisper in his ear, as my body moves closer to his.

Our symbolic first kiss is neither as grand and opulent as depicted in the painting, The Kiss by Gustav Klimt, nor seated, like Rodin's sculpture, but rather it is simple, heartfelt and real. Our kiss will be imprinted on my heart with fulfilling each sense that I feel. The taste of his kiss is as sweet as honey and hot sauce all wrapped into one sensational feeling. Our kiss is a kiss that can build dreams, just like Louis Armstrong sings in the song, "A kiss to build a dream on". My heart is so full of Stephen's kisses that I never want to stop, as the future is in the sweetness of his soft lips. His incredible lips play with every single one of my passions in an irresistible and titillating way. A sincere and intimate moment has fallen upon us. The seductive energy is surreal, almost like a fairytale movie, but this is my reality come true. Perhaps, there is hope after all. I need to have an open mind and heart that he could actually be the one.

Time stands still in that moment of pure blissful kissing. The hands of time escape us as we were embodied in our connection. Stephen slides his nose against my nose and we move to eskimo kissing. He presses his nose and upper lip against mine. Intimately, he breathes in, which allows my skin to be suctioned in by his upper lip. The sensation of our faces rubbing and touching softly has my heart racing, like I'm a high school girl all over again. He touches my face with his fingertips, gently following my jawline, he lifts my chin, opens his eyes and melts me with his biggest, warmest smile.

"Sammie, You are beautiful both inside and out."

He pulls me close.

"You know I would admire you no matter what."

"And you are simply amazing." I respond.

"You could wear your pajamas and no make-up and I would still think that you are cool." Stephen continues.

I'm dancing on clouds and gaze at him.

"Thank you."

I find it hard to come out with the right words to express how amazing I'm feeling. Taking it all in, I stare at him to take a mental picture of happiness. This time I'm not going to run or hide from the pure emotion that fills my heart.

Out of the blue, Stephen asks, "What is the craziest thing you have ever done?"

I laugh for a moment. In the last month I've done all sorts of crazy things and been in positions that I never imagined possible. Until being asked, I never really thought long and hard about my actions, or tried defining them. I lived for the moment. I think that discovering my boundaries and limits were part of the process. A moment of transition in my life, redefining who I am and what I can handle. For a while I completely lost my identity, finding myself open to new sensations and situations that I would never have previously contemplated. Stephen looks at me for an answer and I realize that my head has been taken away from the moment.

"Oh that's a very hard question to easily answer," I tell him.

"Sammie, I can tell you are unique and by no means a simple person."

His blazing eyes are solid on me.

"What I can tell you is that I'm dealing with a personal journey of discovery, in who I am and what I want."

His eyes began to crinkle.

"Sammie, I love what I see so far and know that I'm not going to treat you like your past," he says.

It's hard as hell to trust my instincts and know that this guy really cares and is genuine. I give him another soft sweet kiss as if to say, thank you for believing in me and having the confidence to break down my walls and not run. He smiles and knows that the feeling is mutual. He speaks right to my heart without saying a word. The unspoken words I hear are that he needs me as much as I need him. He will catch me and guide me through the rest. The night ends in mystery but moves forward with promise.

The next day, I'm lying alone lazily in my own bed. It seems like forever since I last had a moment where I stayed in bed so long, just ironing the sheets with the warmth of my body. The morning sun beams in, lighting the room. Quietly relaxing, I'm comfortable in my own skin and loving who I am. I am coming to terms with all that I've seen, done and experienced, and I'm neither afraid nor ashamed. They have made me a richer person. Stephen is right. I am beautiful both inside and out. I'm not a model, I may not have an amazing figure, tiny booty, or flat stomach, but I am me. I rarely ever felt beautiful and truly loved by those that touched me. Stephen has awoken my heart and reminded me that there are genuine, caring and compassionate people out there. He's a true gem, worth more than his weight in gold.

My journey of self-discovery has enabled me to explore and expand my comfort zones. Finding acceptance in who I am and what I stand for is something that I needed to figure out. However, there is still something missing from my life. I still need to identify my main purpose and define my calling. Stephen has managed to do this by joining the Bay Preservation Society.

What can I do to make a difference? I need to have a clear picture and plan, and put it into action. I put on stretchy black pants and a sweatshirt, get into my car and drive. I'm not really sure of my destination but I'm hoping for a sign. Sometimes I just have to let life happen, and accept the direction in which it takes me.

As I'm driving, I see a yoga studio. Sure, I can dance and do limited aerobics, but I've never tried yoga before. What have I got to lose by giving it a go? I pull up in the parking lot, and step inside a spacious airy studio. A friendly-faced dark haired woman with an "instructor" badge on her lapel greets me.

"Hi, welcome! My name is Jane. Are you here for the yoga class? If so, you're in luck! We have a class that's just about to start," she says energetically.

"Hi, I'm Sammie. Umm, yeah, sure, although I've not really tried it before," I say slightly apologetically, feeling a little out of my league.

"Don't worry Sammie, we have students of all abilities. We'll walk you through the main positions at your own pace," she happily replies.

"Our arm balance and inversion workshop will help you free your body, mind and spirit. We'll teach you core strengthening poses and key fundamentals for lift off. It will help you to focus your thoughts in a peaceful manner, that will allow your mind to relax. Would you like to join us?"

I laugh at the very thought.

"Yeah, that sounds cool, why not! I'll give it a try!"

She smiles and signs me up, there and then, before I have a chance to change my mind.

I'm led into another room where there are around a dozen other people, of all shapes and sizes, patiently waiting for the class to begin. As I enter, they turn to greet me with hellos, immediately making me feel welcome and at ease. I take my place at one of the vacant floor mats, and await Jane's instruction and direction.

Standing tall with my feet together, shoulders relaxed, and weight distributed evenly throughout my entire body, Jane demonstrates and describes the movements and yoga positions for Crow Poses, Firefly, Scissors, and several others with equally strange names that I've never heard of. She explains that these positions open the body's energy channels and psychic center. I'm participating and being physically challenged at the same time, but I give it my best shot. She focuses my mind on my breathing, telling me how to breath and how to relax. With a few alignment cues, I'm ready to go.

I direct all my energies to my center, keeping still and steady while relaxing and retaining body control, and it starts to feel good, real good. The serene atmosphere and calm environment allows me to concentrate on the movements of my body and to close my mind to both internal and external distractions. She talks about living a centered life. It's a meditative experience which heightens my senses, not just around my sexy bits, but my entire body. I'm learning to exercise mind over matter. I scan my entire body to make sure that I'm relaxed from head to toe. It's invigorating, energizing, calming, stabilizing and surrendering all rolled into one experience. It's something that allows me to relax and to get in touch with my inner self.

My fears begin to release as I become more in touch with myself. An hour quickly passes by as she reinforces new breathing techniques which help me in processing emotions, feelings, relieving stress, and developing concentration. I look into the mirror at my reflection. I'm far from being a model, but I stand tall with curves and all. My smile shines through more than it did before, and funnily enough, I like what I see in front of me. I'm hooked!

When the class ends, I know that this is something that I need to continue to pursue, in my quest for rediscovery. I think of Nickolaus and the advice he gave me on how to love myself, and smile.

"How did you like your first yoga class?" Jane asks afterward.

"I loved it!," I reply. "I had no idea how challenging or fulfilling it would be."

"That's great Sammie! I'm glad that you enjoyed your experience. I hope to see you again soon!"

"Definitely! Thanks Jane!"

On my way out, I decide to call my best friend to invite her over, since we haven't caught up in ages. Maria always picks up on the first ring, never screening her calls like I do. The phone rings once and she picks up.

"Hey girl! I don't suppose you would like to come on over would you? I've so much to catch up with you," I say.

It's funny how we can go for months on end without seeing one other, but our friendship is such that we just pick up from where we both left off. No questions asked and no drama. I don't have to pretend to be someone that I'm not with her. She's the one person in my life that never asks where I am and what takes me so long in getting back to her. We both understand that life is too short for falling out over petty stuff. In my circle of friends, Maria understands, loves and accepts me for who I am. She always tells me to believe in myself and find the princess within. She's right, and I don't know why it took me so long to listen.

"Hola mi querido amigo! That sounds like a plan. I can swing by around fiveish. What d'ya think?" she says in her thick Spanish accent.

"Great! Looking forward to it." I reply.

Maria and I connected a very long time ago. We were unlikely friends, but found commonality while working together at the salon. Like me, she is also a survivor of domestic violence. Although I found it hard to reveal all of my secrets at first, because of her own experiences, she understood the unspoken pain that I'd endured over the years.

We are unconventional friends from different backgrounds and cultures who share the same spiritual beliefs. She is Puerto Rican, and her strength and dominance are the qualities I most admire about her personality. Maria tells it like it is and never holds back. Like Buzz and Woody, we will remain friends forever, through thick and thin.

My yoga experience is influencing me to make more positive internal and external changes. Mind, body and spirit coming together as one. I'll improve my diet and focus on myself with a greater sense of love, connection, and peace. Food will nourish my body and soul. I decide that I'll serve a nice Mexican grain salad with a versatile combination of ingredients. Tonight, I'll use quinoa, pinto beans, kidney beans, corn, bell peppers and brown rice, spiced up with some chili powder, cayenne pepper, and garlic. Olive oil and red wine vinegar to add to the flavor, and last but not least, some cilantro and just a pinch of salt.

While making this healthy meal, I feel like a new inspired me. I sing along to the music of "It's my Life" by Bon Jovi really loudly in my living room, while shaking and grooving around, singing even louder to the chorus, as it plays over the radio.

Damn it! I'm Sammie and I'm proud! I may have more fat than I should, but that's just fine.

Music has permeated my life, making itself a backdrop to my life, following me through both the good and bad times. Music keeps me company and follows me wherever I go. It has been there in my darkest days, being my saving grace when I had little left to grasp to for help. The voices of my favorite artists singing their songs to me with their inspiring lyrics, helping to lift my spirits, or change my perception. Without music in my life, I would have been lost a long time ago. I now understand why I get together with my friend to enjoy a meal and break some bread, with interesting thoughts and provoking conversation. Like the effect music has on my life, my friend's words inspire me beyond belief.

Where I once saw no hope, I now see new beginnings. Old habits are hard to break, but this time I'm determined to learn from them. I acknowledge and accept the path that I've taken and the ingredients that I've chosen. Recent events have allowed me to grow and develop into a middle-aged woman who now begins to understand herself, but this time the message has changed within. I'm not the same person, I was before my story unfolded.

I open the knocked door, and there stands Maria, a huge smile on her face. She comes in and we give each other a big hug.

Her eyes open wide as she scans my changed appearance and notices my newly-found confidence. She sees the transformation in the woman standing before her. The old Samantha Fleming is dead, a newer fresher version replacing her. The recipe is the same but the ingredients have changed. Metamorphosis complete.

"Now what am I to do with my life?" I ask Maria.

"Oh, Sammie, Surely there must be something you can do with yourself? It's Saturday night and you have no kids in this three-bedroom home of yours in the burbs."

She gestures at my modest empty home. Her optimism always guides me in the right direction. She has a nurturing soul. She remembers the challenges that I've faced. I glance around the room in quiet reflection and notice the silence in facing the realization of my new life. Unlike Dorothy in The Wizard of Oz, I'm not back in Kansas, but I'm sitting in my own house in Newport.

I've had the positive influences and angel voices that encouraged me and watched me grow along my journey. My faith has always been there, but sometimes not realized or valued enough, and at other times simply taken for granted. Faith stands tall beside me even when I'm not looking or aware. I've encountered negative influences which have led me into the wilderness, but somehow I've escaped, enriched by those experiences. I now live my life with no regrets. My life has changed and, for me, this is just the beginning.

Each passing day is giving me a wider appreciation of who I am and who I'm becoming. I've redefined myself and thanks to the 5 C's Challenge, I've tested myself in ways that I never could have imagined. This is my life, and the experiences I've had are real. Love is the main ingredient in my life, and has been the most important in my journey. I'm confident to say that finally, I've learned to discover, be proud of, and genuinely love myself.

ABOUT THE AUTHOR

My P asked about whether I was going to write an "About the Author" page.

"Exciting times for you, dear author!" he said with a smile.

I never really felt I was an author until I saw those words. Of course, I always dreamed and thought there was a very remote possibility.

My profession was one that dealt with people and travel. I also had many other "odd jobs" along the way. However, they were not my true passions in life.

On my own journey, I had the harsh words from an ex who made me feel insecure in my own skin and I had my own obstacles to deal with in life. I became a single parent of three lovely children.

However, inspiration comes in many forms, from the people that you meet along the way to a continuing education course in compulsive gambling I took a few years ago. While I sat in the back of the room, I daydreamed about my life and the entire outline of "Sammie's story" hit me hard.

I believe that it was a gift and I was ready to become an author. I can do this!

Thank you for reading my first novel, and being a witness to my dream!

www.ingramcontent.com/pod-product-compliance
Lightning Source LLC
Chambersburg PA
CBHW060935180626
46817CB00004B/1556